OUT ACROSS THE NOWHERE

OUT ACROSS *the* NOWHERE

Stories by

Amy Willoughby-Burle

Press 53
Winston-Salem

Press 53, LLC
PO Box 30314
Winston-Salem, NC 27130

First Edition

Cover design by Kevin Morgan Watson

Cover art, "Fireflies in a Jar," Copyright © 2012
by Kevin Adams, used by permission of the artist.
www.kadamsphoto.com

Author photo by Matthew Tuers

Library of Congress Control Number: 2012909932

Printed on acid-free paper
ISBN 978-1-935708-60-5

For my family and friends

ACKNOWLEDGMENTS

The author wishes to thank the editors of the publications where the following stories first appeared:

"Bottle Caps and Spanish Gypsies," *Cuivre River Anthology*, 2005

"The Conspicuous Absence of Knowing," *Cuivre River Anthology*, 2009

"The Downside of Redemption," *Reed Magazine*, 2009

"Hungry," *Saltwater Quarterly*, Spring 2011

"The Interring of What Remains," *Quite Curious Literature*, Spring 2011

"Into the Burn," *Inkwell*, Fall 2007

"Limbo," *Artichoke Haircut*, Spring 2012

"Missing Maya," *Sycamore Review*, Winter/Spring 2005

"Nobody Next Door" *Stoneboat, October 2011*

"Out Across the Nowhere," *Summerset Review*, Spring 2009

"Rotten Oranges," *Potomac Review*, Fall/Winter 2004/2005

"Stepping Out in Front of the Train," *Pennsylvania English*, Fall 2007/ Spring 2008

"Stone Jesus in the Front Yard," *MacGuffin*, Fall 2007

"Out Across the Nowhere" won First Prize in the Flash Fiction category of the 2010 Press 53 Open Awards.

OUT ACROSS THE NOWHERE

Stone Jesus in the Front Yard

Concrete and pebbles, tall as a toddler, stone Jesus lays face down in the front yard. This means that our mother is gone. How it means that we don't know. It just does.

My little tow-headed sister and I sit in the living room and watch cartoons. She peeks out the front window to spy on stone Jesus.

"He's still sleeping," she says and lets the sheers drift back into place. "Why is it so quiet in here?"

I turn the television up. My little sister nods her head and sits back down beside me.

When the commercial about the mommy pouring the cereal on the first day of school comes on, my sister and I go outside. We heave stone Jesus to his feet, brush the dirt from his face and wait to see if our mother will come back home.

Stone Jesus is patient. But we give her until the sun rises over the side of the house and then we figure she's not coming back. We make a picnic, spread out an old orange blanket, fix ourselves and stone Jesus a peanut butter and jelly sandwich. We hold it up to his mouth and make eating noises for him. He likes blackberry jelly the best.

At the picnic we tell stone Jesus what we did. Forgive us Father for we have sinned.

"I didn't finish my pork chops and I made my mother cry," I say. "Now you say what you did," I tell my little sister.

"I don't know," she says and shrugs her shoulders.

"You put the hairbrush in the toilet."

"Oh yeah," she says to stone Jesus. "I'm sorry."

He forgives us.

We drag stone Jesus to the edge of the drive. Face him down the road. He can watch for her from here, let us know when she's coming back. Next door, we hear Mrs. Eldon talking to her dog. Her husband is riding around their tiny yard on his riding mower. The man across the street has a push mower that Mrs. Eldon says only works if he doesn't wear his shirt. Our mother would wave at the man across the street when he mowed without his shirt on. The man across the street would smile and wave back. My mother didn't cry on the days the man across the street mowed without his shirt on.

"Maybe he knows where she went," my sister says and points at the house across the street.

"Why would he know?" I say kind of mean and run back across the yard to the swing set. Inside the house, my mother's closet is empty and her new hairbrush is gone from the bathroom sink. Once, at the grocery, when my mother sent me back a few aisles for saltines, I heard Mrs. Eldon say she had never seen a woman so in need of something as my mother.

When the sun slips between the oak and swing set, we decide to dress stone Jesus up like a snow man. We put a cap on him, it's purple with a butterfly on it. We wrap a pink scarf around his neck. He looks pretty good. By dusk, stone Jesus is tired of wearing the cap and scarf so we take them off him. We chase fireflies around the yard. One lights on stone Jesus' head like a little green halo.

All day our mother's car is in the garage. All day the red pick-up truck across the street is gone.

"I bet she will bring us back a present," my tiny sister says, "like when daddy went to Mexico and sent us each a doll."

I take my little sister by the shoulders and hold her still in front of me.

"Mommy bought those dolls at the dime store."

Made in Mexico is stamped on their little plastic butts.

"But daddy," she starts, then understands there is no reason to continue.

"Daddy didn't go to Mexico. He just went away."

"Oh," my sister says and nods her head. "Ok."

When the stars come out we drag stone Jesus back into the yard, lay our heads at his feet and look up into the sky. We trace out pictures like connect the dots. When we get sleepy, we push stone Jesus over on his back, snuggle down on either side of him and pray, Now I lay me down to sleep, I pray stone Jesus my soul to keep. If I should die before I wake, I pray stone Jesus my soul to take. We laugh, but it's not really funny.

It gets cold and my little sister starts to cry. Please, stone Jesus, I whisper in his ear, please bring our mother back before the air gets still and the night gets loud, before she forgets she left us here.

I reach over stone Jesus, put my hand on my sister's arm and sing to her.

Jesus loves you this I know, for the Bible tells me so, little ones to him belong, they are weak but he is strong. She stops crying.

My little sister turns on her side and puts her arm across stone Jesus' chest. She reaches back out for my hand. A dog whines in the distance and we hold our breath.

"Do you think he's cold," she says of stone Jesus.

"Maybe," I say.

I get the picnic blanket and cover the three of us over. My little tow-headed sister falls asleep and I listen for a pick-up truck on the black top. I hear cicadas and see a bat fly over; I hear that dog in the distance and the other dog he's calling to. I think I drift off to sleep because I see my mother making breakfast and crying and the man with the push mower knocking on the door and the very first smile my mother wore in years and I see my little sister and me growing invisible—calling out to someone who is forgetting the sound of our voices.

Later I feel the sun rising, hear birds and bugs and everything in the out-there that is still here with us. When my sister is awake, we raise stone Jesus to his feet. We brush the dirt from the back of his head, sit beside him and tell him all the things he already knows.

Out Across the Nowhere

Summer is the easiest time to slip away—when they're drunk on amaretto sours and each other and they forget all about us. Nights like this, when the two of them are crowded up with company and the world is buzzing around them, my brother and I are like little lost boys, set free out in a world full of magic and abandon. We see our parents and their party like a photograph of a celebration—all grins and grace—time stopped just before the moment it all falls apart.

The fat moon is orange and the craters on the surface make it look like a jack-o-lantern in the sky. It's July though, and the leaves and grass are thick and green and the night is swollen with little noises. Ash sifts down from burned up fireworks exploding in the park. The green and blue and whizzy white all used up and over with. That's how fast it all turns gray.

We leave our parents and their friends to fend for ourselves as we have come to do. We run off to our own place—down the hill and through the patch of tiger lilies like little orange campfires, past the horses that aren't ours, to where the stand of trees in the way-back is lit up with fireflies. So many of them it looks like all the stars have left the sky to come roost in the tree limbs. We climb the branches and try to pluck a handful, hot and twinkling on our fingers. We could swallow them and make little galaxies in our empty stomachs.

We hear laughing from our house, so small and white in the distance. Up there in that world, dark silhouettes toss bottle rockets and swirl sparklers through the night, thinking they've caught a star on a stick. Making wishes in a panic. The yard fills with short lived light and we're out under the forever, far enough in the distance to see how easily magic can die. We wonder if later, after their guests have stumbled away, will our parents call out to us, We're going to bed, be good, don't stay up too late.

Will they know we aren't there?

In the firefly tree, a light, hot wind rolls the leaves against each other in a sound like a song from above a cradle. It's a whisper that goes back further than we do, further even than the dark silhouettes in our yard. Back all the way to the first days of this tree, the first time two leaves touched and the wind carried off their secrets on her back. Now, the tree is ancient and sturdy with knowledge. Its arms are able to support the weight of our wonder and sadness.

Two white cats from next door circle our pond. We follow them around the greened over water and wonder, if our parents looked back and saw us, would they recognize us—yell, what are you doing out there? Get in here and go to bed. Or would they stumble over themselves in laughter, down another sour and rail about how the neighbor cats look big as kids out in the distance.

Doesn't someone around here have kids that size?

They mean well. They think they see the world

around them as sages do, wizened with drink and time. We don't hold their helplessness against them. They didn't mean for all this to happen. They meant to look for us when we got lost. We made our own map instead.

Enough times out the back door, down Tiger Lily Hill, through the Pasture of the Unknown Horses, and to the Milky Way Tree and we will find it. Our portal into the other world. The world of bedtime stories and cookies for dessert. We believe it's there. We must.

Over the tree line into the park, the finale booms. One last shot to make it all mean something. The horses swish their tails at the ash the way they do the flies. We hold our hands out to catch the ash like a bubble, try to nudge it back into the air without breaking it. Some things are tougher than you think. Most of them aren't. They break just like you thought they would.

We sit on the bank of the pond, poke sticks in the green water and watch the party wind down like someone turning the volume lower and lower on the TV. Finally our parents do go inside. Lights come on in the kitchen where our mother will be putting her glass in the sink, they go off and light comes on again down the hall, then their bedroom where they will sleep it off till morning. No light appears in our room.

We sneak up into the yard, like time travelers— peeking into their party without them knowing we were there. We imagine we are in the photograph. They are captured, still. Our parents, their heads slightly back with faces framed in laughter, hold drinks in one hand and stars in the other. Their guests, some crouch over a bottle rocket—flame suspended, anticipation hot in the air. Others sit in lawn chairs, gazing at the fireworks just visible over the distant tree line. We run through the yard, the only things in motion. We circle the burned spot in the grass where launch and applause have scorched the ground. We run between the lawn chairs, imagining we can obstruct views, elicit yells and calls of "shoo kid" — there is nothing but silence.

Inside our parents are sleeping. Our father snores, thick noise like a bear and we laugh at hearing it through the wood and windows. We sit for a moment, my brother and me, in the chairs in the yard. We listen for the snoring to stop and for footsteps to begin searching the house for us. But in the house, our parents continue to slumber while in the next room our little beds get smaller and smaller. After some time, my brother rises, nods to me and I follow him back through the yard, back down Tiger Lily Hill, through the Pasture of the Unknown Horses, and again to the Milky Way Tree, where under the pumpkin moon, the little kids out across the nowhere, with their bellies full of stars, are getting farther and farther away.

THE CONSPICUOUS ABSENCE OF KNOWING

I'm in a Texaco men's room pinching back the first nosebleed I've had since I was ten. Everything is stark and unnatural. The smells of urine and industrial strength soap seep around the reality that my father has died. Locked out of the ladies room, I stand here, head bent forward, realizing that this is the same Texaco men's room my father took me to almost thirty years ago, when before we had even left town on a trip to Disney World, my nose began to bleed. When it happens to other people, this is the sort of irony that I usually enjoy. Today it turns the whole world pale.

I hear the toilet flush in the ladies room next door and I swear that it's my mother all those years ago, wearing that orange, flower-print mini dress that came to her knees because she was so short; carrying that big white wonder purse that held all the necessities of childhood. How strange it was that it was my father who took care of me that day.

"Just hold your head back," he said closing a tissue around my nose.

Thick metal slid down the back of my throat, salt dripped down my cheeks.

"You're ok." He patted the top of my head. "This used to happen to me all the time. It's nothing to worry about."

The toilet flushed in the ladies room and I knew my mother and my little sister, Lola, were outside waiting for us.

"It won't last long," he continued to reassure me. "You'll forget this ever happened."

Now I sit here in that Texaco and close my eyes around the memory of the sweet soda that my father bought me after the bleeding stopped and of the handful of peanuts that he gave me once we were all back in the car, peanuts from his jar, Daddy's jar. The world warps out of perspective and for a minute I remember the magnitude of what a small pleasure like that can mean to a child.

For six months before his death my father had been in a nursing home. For five days of that time he had known who I was. Not five days in a row, just five days. On the last day that he remembered me, he looked up from his pureed dinner and said in his regular voice, a voice I hadn't heard in a while, "It's ok, Peanut, the food will be much better where I'm going. I won't even remember I was here." Two days later he left us.

Jack didn't go with me to collect my father's things. This was the first sign that it wouldn't work out between us. A young man in blue scrubs, with a nametag that read "Zane — Nurse's Aid" helped me load all the belongings and take them out to my car. I'd seen him around. He worked the hall my father was on. What a weird job, I had thought, caring for these people you can't possibly make well.

I cried, as I'm sure all people loading items into their trunk off the gray, metal cart do. It was nothing that

Zane hadn't seen before. He hugged me and I thought of kissing him hard on the mouth like some desperate woman, twenty years older than he, clinging on to something that he didn't understand.

"I'm sorry," I said, fearing I had held on too long.

"Don't be," he said. "You're sad. We're sad too."

"Thank you."

He nodded and I closed the trunk over my father's things.

Once I'm back in the car, nosebleed over, Jack calls.

"Look, I think I should be there with you," he says. "Funerals are hard."

I'm not sure that he has a place in the middle of my sadness. I don't know that I want him to see in that far.

"I'd like that."

This is a lie and a test.

"Let me see if I can move some things around," he says.

Typical stall. He'll call back in about thirty minutes and tell me he has a meeting that he just can't move, try as he might. He'll blame some of it on his business partner and say something along the lines of—this is a time you should be with your family, you don't need me around to worry over—trying to make me feel like he's giving me space, being understanding of my feelings.

Total bullshit.

"That's fine," I say. "Call me later."

When my cell rings again it's Lola.

I dread my little sister the most. I keep calling her that although we're women, grown, schooled, married, mistaken, on our own. Today though, she'll be little again. I will be too, but I'll hold it together so I can help her heart as it breaks. I can do that for her. For all the things I couldn't do, so much as I wanted, this one thing, I can.

"Hello." I answer knowing that she's called to ask me something that seems off subject, trivial. She does that when she's about to fall apart.

"Hey, Sissy," she says, and the use of that long ago nickname makes the road blur.

"Are you with Mom?" I keep the tears out of my voice.

"Yes," she says. "Look, do you remember that guy, Steve, with the lawnmower, from when we were little."

"Sure." I don't understand the diversion so far, but it means she's not handling this well.

"What did we call him?" she asks.

That was the summer that the Pulous's across the street had an exchange student from Russia. Stefan. They called him Steve. We called him Prev. Our mother never said an undesirable word in front of us. She would pronounce things slightly off kilter so that pervert was prevert. That sort of thing.

Prev mowed our lawn for free that summer. He had a crush on Lola. He never minded that she wore a brace on her ankle. She was thirteen and most boys had stopped noticing the brace altogether. She was becoming beautiful from the inside out. When she got the brace off a few years later, no one even remembered it had been there. I still see it glinting on her leg, even now sometimes.

All that summer, Prev had stood outside her window and tried to spy her getting dressed, watched her sleeping, scared the piss out of her when she noticed it.

"We called him Prev," I remind her.

"Oh yeah," she says and laughs. "Remember when Prev was shining his flashlight in the window and you held up that record cover with that demon guy on it—who was that guy—and he fell backwards into that spiky, ugly plant Mom had by the tree."

It was Dad's record. He used to play this game where he snuck into our room and made these zombie noises, holding that album cover up to his face to scare us. We screamed and hid under the covers. Our little hearts pounding, fear squealing out of us even though we knew it was all make-believe and magic.

We loved that game.

"I remember," I say.

"Are you far away?"

She needs me.

"I'm almost there."

At the nursing home, my father's roommate was called Cricket. Cricket Cole. He had Parkinson's and a wild imagination brought on by the drugs that came around at timed intervals. The medicine stopped his body from shaking and sent his mind reeling. He told me the room was filled with dogs. Asked me if I liked dogs, if the barking bothered me.

"They're not really here," Cricket would say. "I see them, but they're not real. I wish they wouldn't bark so loudly, though."

A young woman came to visit him on Thursdays. She brought him a chocolate milkshake from McDonald's and he told her stories from his life before now. I was never sure who she was. Not his daughter, but she seemed to love him. He wanted her to park his Cadillac outside so that he could go for a drive sometime. She said she would, just as soon as she got it filled with gas. He was hard to understand, the disease taking his clarity of speech, but she understood every word. They laughed and told each other jokes.

I had always envied them. I had envied everyone really. The nurses and aides, the physical therapist, the people visiting from church on Sundays—they could walk out into the sunlight and air and leave it all behind.

Cricket had been there when I collected Dad's things. I guess he had lost roommates before.

"Did I tell you about the time the room was full of pigs?"

I shook my head, kept packing.

"Well, it was filled up with them. I hid in the bathroom. Nate just kept saying 'Pull the emergency light, Cricket. Pull the light.' But I was too scared of the pigs."

I had finally come to understand Cricket's slurred speech, to understand exactly what he was saying. To see exactly how much he missed Dad too.

"What I liked about Nate was that he didn't say 'snap out of it Cricket, there are no pigs.' He just tried to help me get someone in here to get rid of them. I know there weren't any pigs. He knew it too."

I had been determined not to cry. My determination was failing.

"He knew when you were here," Cricket said, looking out the window. "He knew you."

Maybe they had some secret language, Cricket and Dad. Dad not saying much of anything and Cricket always talking but barely understood. All day they sat in that room. Under the medicine and beyond the oxygen machines, outside the bing bing of the call bells and noises from the nurses' station, what did they know?

Some secret truth of what happens next?

The cell rings again. It's Jack. I'm right about everything I thought he'd say and it makes me oddly happy. It makes this whole thing easier.

"Look, Jack," I say. "I don't have room for this."

"Room for what?" he answers and I hear that someone is talking to him in his office. "I'll make that top concern," he says to someone else.

"Anyway," I say, "I'm with someone new now." This is a lie.

"Really," he says, suspecting as much, "who?"

"Zane," I say, shocked at myself. "I met him at the nursing home when you wouldn't come with me to get Dad's things. We made out in the parking lot."

"On the day you picked up your Dad's things?"

"Why not? And he's about twenty years old, maybe younger. Maybe I broke the law even, who knows."

"And you're dating this guy?"

"Sure. He's off on Wednesdays and we spend all day in the backseat of the car."

"You're lying."

"Not about all of it."

He sighs and I ride down the road with the phone to my ear, saying nothing, hearing less. After a minute I just hang up.

I had been having lunch with an old college friend when the Charge Nurse had called to tell me that my father was dying. I had excused myself, saying I needed to get back to the office — that something was wrong with the layout and I needed to speak to one of our photographers. It was an elaborate lie for no good reason. She'd find out soon enough that my father had passed away, but I couldn't let her in at that moment. A chronic problem of mine.

"I'm sure everything will be fine," she said as we paid our bill and gathered ourselves to leave. "You have a knack for fixing things."

"I don't know if I can fix this."

"Sure you can," she said, with no idea what we were really talking about. "You're like Wonder Woman."

I pull up in front of my mother's house, noticing the very precise spacing of tulips edging the walk to the front door. Mom has a knack for that sort of control over things that spring from the ground. I envy that level of mastery over the world around her. Truth be told, I guess, it's all a cover-up. Pretty though, all the pink and white. I get out and just stand there by the car. Laughter leaks from the open windows in the house that holds my childhood. It's that sort of laughter born from the exhaustion of heartbreak and it makes me ache for what's not possible.

I close the car door. There is no way to get out of this. There's no way not to walk, determined, to the front door, no way not to turn the knob and go inside, no way not to cross the threshold of what was into what will be.

Limbo

I t's not so much what he says as the way he says it—
low and soft so you have to lean in, so that everything
is intimate, so that should this be the last of it, you pull
away with his breath in your ear like a passenger from
where he's stuck to wherever you're going. Perhaps to
the Thai place on the corner with the peanut noodles you
always get and the coconut chicken that he loves but can't
swallow anymore. Or to the pub on the corner where he
orders a Fat Tire and you get whatever is the darkest
brew they have. Even one that makes him laugh because
it's black as motor oil. No matter, you're an unwilling
taxi service with his voice in your ear and going on with
it all seems cruel and pointless.

Out in the world there's a lady in the grocery who
curses you out for being in the express lane with eleven
items when the sign clearly says "ten or less" so you
take a can of biscuits off the belt and toss it back toward
the aisle from whence it came. It pops open when it hits
the floor, startling a stocker who knocks over the holiday
display of Keebler cookies he'd just finished stacking
into the shape of a Christmas tree.

"You should clean that up," the lady says to you.

"Merry Christmas," you say to her and she rolls her eyes.

When you were younger the universe had rules. If you rolled a six, you moved six spaces and you followed whatever directions you were given. If you got tagged you were out. If you made it back to base you were safe. Now things don't work that way.

On the fourth floor of the hospital it's still Halloween despite the peel off quote-of-the-day calendar which proclaims the twentieth of December and that "This too Shall Pass." A plastic Jack-o-lantern at the nurse's station smiles its snaggle-toothed grin at you as you wait for the nurse to finish her routine blood draws and machine checks. When she walks back to the desk you're looking at the little wooden skeleton sitting on top of the computer. She giggles apologetically and puts it in her pocket.

"We really should put up a tree or some lights," she says going on about her business. "It looks like death around here."

In his room someone has turned on an old spy movie because they don't know him well enough to know he'd prefer whatever is showing on SyFy. The television is in the far upper corner of the room but the sound comes from speakers on the bed rails.

The gap between the sense of sight and sound is akin to watching someone translate speech into sign language—making you want to look frantically from the speaker to the hands and back to the speaker again, as if somewhere in the space between them the truth of what's being said might be left out.

Out in the waiting room between visitation times you choose not to join the community of loved ones, the usual faces, the ones just like you. You decline to sit a spell with Aunt Clara from Minnesota who has flown in for what would have been her brother, Ted's, fiftieth birthday celebration. You don't want a piece of the cake they all share in the waiting room. You think it's weird that they brought balloons and paper hats. You try to pass quickly when new people turn up. You don't want to know if the three little girls and the desperate looking man are the family of the woman brought in two days ago. You don't share small talk as you wait for the inner doors to open, you go in first and try not to look at the faces so that you won't know when someone stops coming and you won't have to wonder why.

Once, at the last visiting time of the day, an entire wedding party came in—the bride in a mermaid cut gown and groom in a nicely fit tuxedo, some old ladies in lavender dresses, bridesmaids in sage taffeta— still holding their flowers. You didn't want to look at them either, but you couldn't help yourself.

You live in one of those neighborhoods where people string Christmas lights to every archway and eve, perfectly outlining the contours of their houses. Animatronic deer and Santas and luminaries in white paper bags that you imagine bursting into flame. You weren't in the mood this year but you strung the damn lights anyway to avoid explaining why yours was the only dark house on the block. And who knows, maybe the colored lights and plastic nativity scene will make you smile despite yourself.

On Christmas Eve, as you pull out of the driveway on the way to the hospital, one of the luminary bags in front of Jackie Pressley's house catches fire. The brisk December wind blows the spark to the next bag and the next and the sight of her running from the house, wearing her Mrs. Claus apron and beating the fire with a spatula does, in fact, brighten your day.

At work no one knows. You've never been one to offer up personal information. Your office is like déjà vu of what your life used to be. Water cooler chat, committee meetings, and projects you could complete. It's nice in a way. It's a break. You amaze yourself at your ability to fake it. Everyone is primed for their New Year's Eve celebration and although you enjoy the buzz of an office filled with suits and ties and pointy-toe pumps on the brink of getting off work early to cast their cares away, you know their countdown of three, two, one, toward new possibilities is a silly dream.

You herald the New Year in the hospital. He hasn't spoken in days. So when he asks you to turn off the television you agree although it isn't on. You wonder if he thinks all the noise around him is one of those hospital dramas and you think maybe it is. But it's a rerun. You've seen this one before. It's on every single day. Maybe you could turn on the Spanish translation feature. Maybe in another language it will turn out differently.

For three days you can't get to the hospital because the ice on your windshield is two inches thick and you live on one of the last roads in town to see a plow. The first day you're in a panic. You should be there. You call— no changes. Don't worry they tell you. He'll be fine. That's not what they mean. They mean nothing will change.

Everything is frozen.

The second morning you wake up like a person on vacation. You open the drapes and watch the locals play. The Patterson kids had gotten a new sled for Christmas and since they have the steepest driveway in the neighborhood and the school busses didn't run and there is no danger of passing cars, kids from the woodwork are lined up with their own sleds and trashcan lids and pieces of plywood and you watch them take turns hurling themselves into the biting wind and whip of reckless abandon.

You sip your coffee and remember what it was like to not know how hard the world can beat you down.

On the third day you feel like you've gone to a movie with so many trailers that for a minute, you're unsure what you're there to see. You think long and hard on the matter and after some time you can actually remember how you used to spend your day. You were involved in a local artisans group. You made pottery. You may still have a booth rented at a weekly art fair in town. It's like coming out of a coma. A long amnesia from which the dissolving leaves you heartsick.

You dread doilies and red and pink construction paper. You fear the way they smell like kindergarten and cupcakes. For a few days in early February he talks again. He says things that make sense—not ramblings about the past, but inquiries about noises and needles and you wonder if all this while he has known.

Amidst the cruel linger of winter he gives it up. He feels it's time to "throw in the towel" he whispers to you. You begin the surreal conversations about staying or letting go. You apologize for old injuries to which no apology will suffice, finishing long ago begun conversations that seemed best left open-ended at the time. You listen hard to the sound of his voice, grateful to hear it again after all the silence. You've been strong so far. Hope can make a superhero of the heart. But now, your face is weary from the expense of tears and there seems nothing to do but wait for the last of it.

Winter clings and you figure there is no other season. But everything ends and this will too. Whether you like the outcome or not doesn't much matter. Whether it ends abruptly or just slowly becomes something else is not within your control. You feel like a snowflake who used to be a droplet of water and who but for the frozen ground beneath would melt away again.

MISSING MAYA

She has a tendency to wander off, which is why we didn't miss her until she'd been gone for about two weeks—as best any of us could figure.

One time she'd grown tired of this pseudo-hip 80's dance club we'd all gone to and she'd said to me, "This place blows, Travis. I'm leaving." And we didn't see her for three days.

Turned out she'd met an old friend in the parking lot and the two of them decided to go to the beach. Atlantic City, which is like, hundreds of miles from here, where they—so she said—hit a little bit of a jackpot and spent the whole time ordering double martinis and entertaining at nude hot tub parties in their complementary suite at Trump Plaza.

She had the pictures to back it up too. The two of them, Maya and this mystery girl, bare breasts half submerged in hot water, holding up martini glasses tilted sideways—the martinis spilling into the bubbling water, partygoers looking on and smiling. And another catty-wampus shot of Maya, wearing green striped underwear and no top, someone's hands cupping her breasts from behind, her smiling—mouth wide open, head full of choppy brown hair all out of sorts and everyone's eyes stuck to her like her tan skin was sweet honey.

She passed these pictures out like she didn't give a damn that she was naked. Which she didn't. A friend of mine works at Pisano's Pizza and whenever Maya calls, he says that the drivers fight over her order because she's always answering the door naked and they keep hoping that one day she'll invite one of them in for some porno-quality sex and maybe a shot of whatever she's drinking.

"See," she had said about the Trump Plaza pictures, "this guy here," the one with his hands on her tits, "he works in the casino, got us free drinks."

She always had proof, although she never needed it. We all believed everything she said. Like the time we were all at Denny's and she started going on about forward velocity and Henry Miller and then asked the waitress what time it was and after hearing the reply said that she was late for class and shoved the last of her sandwich in her mouth, grabbed her coat, threw too much money down on the table and left.

So seeing as how she worked double shifts at the Soap and Suds, which is this all-night Laundromat that serves beer and cheese fries, we had no idea what she was talking about. We laughed about that being "typical Maya" and didn't mention it again until she said she couldn't go out one night because finals were the next day and that she was failing physics. So we muscled it out of her that she'd been going to the local university, sitting in on two lit classes and that physics class she was failing and said that she'd have to retake next semester because she needed the credits.

We asked her when she'd enrolled in school and she

said that she hadn't, she just started going. Then she bitched about how one of her lit teachers refused to grade her term paper because she wasn't on his roll chart and that if he was going to be a bastard about it there was no way she was going to meet him at Cubbies for the one-on-one conference he'd requested. Then she'd said, "Which is a shame because I had all intentions of screwing him, if that's what he was after."

One of us asked her once how often she went to these classes and she said "I don't really go that often, I just stole the books from the book store so that I can sell them back at the end of the semester for beer money." We figured that was more like the truth.

But this time, she's got us all worried. She's never been gone this long without at least sending somebody a postcard. Like that time she said she was going to Taco Bell and went to Mexico instead. She had just broken up with Tim and had been craving tacos with extra guacamole—she said the color green made her happy. So when she said she was going to ride her bike through the late-night drive thru—she doesn't have a car—and see if they would serve her, we didn't think anything of it. Jack wanted to ride with her because it was after midnight but she wouldn't let him.

So about 2:30 a.m. when she wasn't back, me and a couple of the other guys walked over to Taco Bell, which was closed by then, to look for her. So we just assumed that we missed her and Jack said, "She's probably back at your place, Travis," and we walked back over to my apartment. Maya lives next door to me.

When we got there we heard this loud music coming from her place and we assumed that she'd gotten her tacos and was home eating away her sorrows. But then a few days later, Lori got a postcard from Mexico and it turned out that it must have been Tim playing the music—he still has a key to her place—because Taco Bell was closed when Maya got there so instead she bought a bus ticket to Mexico where she informed us that the guacamole was much better than at Taco Bell and that she was never going to eat at that hole again.

And that's all the card said: "The guacamole is much better here than at that Taco Bell. I'm never eating at that hole again."

The front of the card said Mexico real big at the top and had a picture of a big blue frog. Nobody understood that. Or where she'd gotten the money to buy a bus ticket to Mexico from here. Or even that you could.

She hadn't said anything about when she was coming back. But after a few more days she called me from the Soap & Suds to ask if I'd come pick her up from work because she was too tired to walk home after the bus ride back. She said that she hadn't gotten any sleep because the guy behind her had kept her awake all night talking about how he couldn't get it up unless the woman gave him head. She said she didn't find out if that was the truth.

So this time we get a hold of the landlord and tell him that we think Maya is missing and ask if he'll unlock the door and let us check things out. At first he gives us a hard time about it but then he seems to realize that if Maya is gone he doesn't get any rent, so he unlocks the door. Tim is asleep on the couch and for a second I forget that he's not supposed to be here. It's been months since they broke up. Months since the "Mexico incident" as we call it. We wake him up and ask what the hell he's doing there and he says he's waiting on Maya and do we know where she is because she's got his physics book and he has a test in two days.

I ask when he started taking physics and he says that he's in Maya's class. No one really gives enough of a damn to go any further with it, we just ask when he saw her last and he says he saw her at work. We all give a sigh assuming he means today, but then he goes on to say, "a couple weeks ago."

Jack asks Tim if he's been here waiting for her all that time and Tim says, "No, jackass, what do I look like, an idiot?" No one comments because it's too easy. Then Lori notices Maya's bike is in the living room. We all start talking like detectives.

—So it stands to reason that she couldn't have gone far or she would have taken the bike.

—From the food left on the stove it's evident she meant to come right back.

—Assuming this food is from two weeks ago and not simply earlier today.

Tim asks what the hell is going on and Jack kicks him out. Speaking of all the cop talk, Jack suggests we call the county lock-up. Maybe this is like the time Maya said over the music at Giddy's that she was going up to the bar and then we didn't see her again.

But when I had gotten home that night the words "Give me head or give me death" were written in neon green paint on my front door and there was a message on my machine from Maya saying that she was drunk and in jail and, no hurry, but when we got around to it could someone come get her out, but that if we weren't coming until in the morning not to come too early because she wanted to sleep in.

Or the time when she got locked up for being drunk at the mall and hitting on the store Santa and she used her one phone call to check her own messages because she was waiting to hear from this guy she met at Giddy's that "looked just like Brad Pitt, or at least from behind." Actually there were quite a few times that she was drunk and locked up come to think of it. It's not that we don't care enough to watch her, it's that she does these things all the time and they usually end up in a funny story that we tell to people who don't know her when she's not in the room and tell to ourselves when she is.

But there have been some stories along the way that weren't so funny. Like the time she was riding her bicycle back from the bar because "cops don't usually stop drunks on bicycles" she had said. She tells the story like this, but the ending of it is actually much different— Giddy's is at the top of a hill and she was coasting to the bottom, but she was too toasted to know she was at the bottom when she got there and never started to peddle again, so the bicycle started to slow down and she couldn't figure out why and thought that it must be out of gas, so she tried to steer it to the gas station at the bottom of the hill and all the while the bicycle was getting slower and slower until it came to a stop and the whole damn thing just fell over with her on it and she was lying there in the street with this rusty Schwinn on top of her, wishing she had filled the tank before she left the bar.

And that's the end of the way she tells it. But the end is actually this—a brown Chevy station wagon tagged her as she was standing the bike up and sent her flying over the hood and into the hospital for days. We didn't know anything had happened until she showed back up with a cast on her arm and a stitched up gash on her head.

So I nod at Lori and she picks up the phone. That's when she sees the message light blinking.

Lori hits play and there's a message from the Soap & Suds about whether or not to put Maya on the schedule for this week seeing as how she didn't come in all last week, and there's one from the police department about some articles that were left in the cell, and then there's one from Maya. She's slurring her words pretty bad and laughing: "Damn, I meant to call Travis. Oh well, they locked me up again and now I'm getting sent to rehab, for Christ's sakes. Sons of bitches. Don't worry, I'll be back. Can somebody give my physics book to Tim so he'll get off my case about it?"

And then there's another one. And she sounds distant and confused. "I can't remember anybody's number," and then there's the sound of her dropping the phone and a mumbled, "Shit, I can't," and that's it.

Jack sits down on the couch and puts a hand over his face. Lori stands frozen, fingers to her mouth in worry. And I'm staring at the message machine like it has all the answers. And it does.

Because then there's another one and this time Maya's crying, "Damn, I meant to call Travis. Anyway, can somebody please bring me something to drink?" and then in the background you can hear somebody yelling about how she's not supposed to be on the phone and she whispers "please, somebody, please." And then she's gone.

Jack stands back up and we all hover over the machine, waiting for more. Only that's it. There is no more. But we stand there for a while looking at it anyway. We all know where she is. And if we were honest, we'd say that we had always known she'd end up there.

So they leave it to me to go see her at the Woodmere Rehab Center and report back. And on the way there I think about the time she was walking down the road lugging a suitcase and I stopped and asked her where she was going and if she needed a ride and she said, "I'm already coming back from where I was going, and anyway I'm almost there."

I wish I had asked her what she was carrying in her suitcase.

I guess that makes all the difference.

Bottle Caps and Spanish Gypsies

A red pickup roars by, stirring up the dry dirt, clouding the air. The rush of hot wind rustles the huge, heavy-headed sunflowers growing wild beside the road. I like sunflowers. The air is thick with the smell of fried food and gasoline and the sound of children begging ice-cream cones while their father refuels the vacation wagon on this stop to somewhere better.

I can see the heat waves in the air. It's that hot. Like the whole damn world is being bar-b-qued. I'm sitting on the hood of our old blue Chevy and the heat from the metal is burning my ass right through my shorts. It feels good though. I wait for a breeze, but one never comes.

My clothes are sticking tight to my skin and my shaggy brown hair is matted to the back of my neck. Sitting here on the car, I watch Payton wash his face at the spigot outside the gas station. Over and over, he cups water into his hands and splashes it over his skin, closing his eyes and holding his face to the sun each time.

He's wearing the same pair of faded jeans that he wore the day I met him. That and nothing else. Not even shoes. I watch the water drip off his face and roll across his chest

31

and down the flat of his belly. On his shoulder, he has a tribal type tattoo that winds down his arm and curves around his bicep. He sees me looking at him and winks.

Having spent the last of our money on a tank of gas, we're just hanging around until the store is busy enough for Payton to walk off with a few things for us to eat. I'm just to wait here at the Chevy. The one Payton says is his. The one I know isn't. But it doesn't really matter.

When I was ten, my father told me that if you get off the bus at the wrong stop you'd do better to get right back on and go where you meant to go, but if the bus has already left you, you might as well go in, get a cup of coffee and get to know the place. All I remember thinking when he'd finished talking was that I was too young to drink coffee. I figured it had something to do with my mom leaving us, but at the time I wasn't sure what. You never know what any of that stuff means when you're ten years old. Hell, I'm twenty- two and I still don't know.

All I do know, is that I don't give a rat's ass about Art History anymore and now that my Dad has Gloria, he doesn't seem to give much of a rat's ass about me. Ok, that's not true. I know the man loves me. He's just preoccupied and happy. And good for him.

So here it was August, and I was on my way back to the college degree I didn't want when I let the bus leave me. So like Dad had said, I went in the first restaurant I saw—Hungry Henry's All You Can Eat Gas and Buffet— and got a cup of coffee. And it was done. Just that easy. I dropped out, disappeared, started over. So that's when I saw this guy standing out in the middle of the parking lot. He was flipping a bottle cap up into the air. He had on old jeans and a blue shirt with a hole in the side and he had the most gorgeous blond hair I had ever seen on a guy. I walked over to him—feeling brave and foolish at the same time.

"Hey," I said.

"What's in the duffel?" he asked, referring to the bag I had strapped over my shoulder. "You hitching?"

"That's none of your business," I said, trying to sound like I had my shit together and that I hadn't just done something rash and terrifying.

"Well, you're the one who walked over here," he said all casual like and looked away.

He had me on that one.

"What's your name," I asked, letting the bag slip off my shoulder.

"Luke," he said and pocketed the bottle cap. "Cool Hand Luke."

"Oh please," I said and rolled my eyes. "You gonna eat fifty eggs in an hour to prove it to me."

He tried to keep a straight face.

"I can," he said.

"Bullshit," I said.

Things didn't end well for Luke and I hoped this guy would fare a bit better. We just stood there looking at each other for a bit. He took the bottle cap out and started flipping it again.

"My name's Payton," he finally said.

"I'm Nikki."

"Nice to meet you, Nik," he said.

I picked up my bag and started to walk away, but he followed after me. When he winked and asked if I needed a ride I almost told him to piss off, but then he ran his hand through that hair of his and I thought, hell, why not.

Payton and I just clicked. Chemistry, he called it. We made love our second night together. Which was probably more like hormones. We took a sheet left out on some old lady's line and laid it down in her yard — moonlight coming through the trees and air smelling like flowers and fabric cleaner.

Since then, we've been driving the highway going nowhere, just hanging around, making love and talking. It feels like I've always been with him. It's been two weeks best I can count.

"Let's go to Spain," he said one night, wrapping his arms around me. "We can join the gypsies."

"How are we going to get to Spain?"

"Drive," he said. "Floor it right over the ocean."

He held my face in his hands and kissed me. Girls really like that shit.

I slide down off the hood of the Chevy when I see Payton go inside the store. When he comes back out his arms are loaded with stuff. He's walking fast and laughing and doesn't so much as glance back over his shoulder, not even once. He tosses the stuff in the back and we hop in the car and pull away. Don't run, he's said, and they won't chase you.

"What'd you get?" I ask and lean over into the back seat to survey the loot.

"Your favorites," he says.

Beanie weenies, salsa, peanuts, some other junk and a six pack of beer. I shake my head. There will be time to learn each other's likes and dislikes.

"I hate this piss," I say about the beer and Payton laughs.

But I'm hot and the beer is cold, and I guess it doesn't taste that bad after all.

"So," he says. "Where do you want to go?"

"Spain," I say and he floors the gas pedal.

He turns up the radio and there's a song playing that

I like. It's about flipping a coin and choosing a new life. It makes me realize something. Something about getting off a bus and into an old Chevy, about getting off the wrong path and onto a better one. It makes me realize that better is in the heart of the beholder.

So days we drive and nights we watch the stars. We don't have much. Just the money we can beg from strangers and a map as worn out from daydreaming as anything else. It doesn't bother me at all that we have nowhere to go and not much to go there for. Right now, it's just the going there that matters.

Payton takes a bottle cap out of his pocket and rolls it between his fingers. I think about the first time I saw him. We pass by another field of sunflowers and Payton points out the Welcome to Arkansas sign.

"We keep heading west and we'll find those Spanish gypsies," he says and winks at me.

"We'll find something," I say.

We'll find what we're looking for when the time is right. Maybe we already have. Payton might not know it, but he is a gypsy in Spain. We both are.

Days Untended

She didn't mean to be sad, she just was. Widowed young, out where the kudzu covered over what might have been. She was backed in by tobacco barns and soybeans and forgotten rows of corn full of spiders and field mice. She longed for the times when the fields burned. Great blazes of freedom, scorching the ground and making it new.

A farm wife in the vast Sampson County piedmont, she had known the time of day by the coming and going of the deer in the peanuts fields. She measured the seasons by seed bud and harvest and passed the years with pen scratches on the wall—marking the three of us girls taller and older. While she worked we filled our afternoons rattling the pecan trees and collecting up enough to make a good sale. We'd catch a ride into Clinton and waste our earnings on Hollywood and buttered popcorn. But that had been back when things were easy.

Once, in the broken moonlight, we watched her slip out into the yard. She kneeled in the spot where she'd found him and put her hands over her face. From the window we watched her shoulders heave—unbearable sobs that shook the whole world.

There'd been a man or three come around to see if he could fill our Daddy's shoes, but she hadn't given any of them a chance. In the kitchen she cooked, wearing a yellow apron and humming some tune from so far back that it made us sad. It must've made her sad too because she paused by the sink and put a hand out to steady herself, even though she was not about to fall.

Some nights we'd catch her huddled in the corner of their closet where she breathed in blue overalls that he once wore, white shirts worn thin, straw hat with a hole in the back of the brim. We planted ourselves like tiger lilies outside her bedroom door when she cried—tried to spread out and make her happy. We were three little girls like stair steps, high enough to raise her up, too small to take her anywhere.

We hadn't known him much as we wanted to. His face always hidden beneath that hat as he climbed the steps of the back porch with the sun nearly set to darkness behind him. His was a kind smile at the dinner table, big rough hands, nails caked with dirt.

Later, we lay waiting in bed for him to poke his head in and kiss our foreheads goodnight. We touched the place his rough lips had pressed and called him, "Daddy, we love you."

When we rambled down the stairs of a morning he'd be out past the cows already or atop his old tractor, weaving in and out of the fields, making do for us. An older man when he married, he worked hard despite his health. Long days in the fields and hot hours in the barns begged he slow down, but he had mouths to feed and a wife to keep.

In the worst of the winters when there was nothing

to do but hope, he would sit in his old chair in the living room and tell us stories of times gone by. In the passing of those gray days, we saw what she saw—his humor and heart and his need for our arms around him as much as we needed it in return. We wished for winter to linger longer, but the sky always turned blue again and we were left without him.

For a time she hired out day workers to tend the fields, but there was not enough harvest to pay them. So the four of us worked what we could, weeded and watered and picked and aimed to keep it going. Once she tried to drive the tractor as he had taught her to, but she couldn't keep her hands on the steering wheel without breaking into those sobs that made us fearful we would lose her too. We managed for a time with what could be tended by hand, but when our school work suffered, she let it all go.

She made use of what grew despite neglect and little spirit for the care of such things. Evenings she'd sit out in the damp— rain like baby-fine mist—and shell beans. She'd hum that old tune and look out toward the dying tobacco fields in the way off. Her hands moved like water over the beans, a rhythm that stilled us and made us lonely.

At dinner, she'd put daises in a blue mason jar atop the orange, flecked Formica table and tune the radio to music older than she. We'd eat golden cornbread, a sliver of pork, and those beans that tasted like heartache so old you couldn't live without it.

With him gone, she made jelly, canned tomatoes, kept busy. She cooked ears of corn and tossed them out the window. She sold the things we could do without, the big clock in the hallway, the covers over the windows, and after a while, the radio and the kitchen table. When our need began to show, the ladies group from the Baptist church had come by with all manner of casserole and cake, but once they figured us taken care of, they moved on to more pressing issues.

We did our best not to need him. Momma tried to stay in the house without him, tried not to reach for him in her sleep, but when there was no more she could do, she scorched the ground.

She moved us to Raleigh where we went to school with kids who didn't know that potatoes grew underneath the dirt. She married a man who worked at the bank. He loved her. We wore nice clothes and on Sundays we piled up for church wearing shiny black shoes and white socks with lace trim. She'd make fried chicken for lunch and sweet tea with mint leaves floating on the ice. In the evening when she washed the dishes, she'd hum that sad song from so far before—her hand gripping the counter, still, to steady herself.

She tried to be happy. Each night she read us stories and kissed our foreheads and we said, "Mommy, we love you."

She said, "You three are the heavens and the seas."

Years later, the bank man died. His heart gave out at his mahogany desk. She told us when we came home from school.

"We're fine," she said, "the four of us."

Although she didn't need the money this time, she took his nice suits to a store in town where you could buy and sell old things. While she waited for the shopkeeper to determine the worth of the fabric and stitches, we rummaged around through the musty contents of the store admiring all the things that someone had once cared for, but could now do without.

"Let's go, girls. We've no more use here."

The three of us trailed behind her, taller this time, though still not able to give her wings. She didn't mean to miss the other one instead, she just did. Nights, she sat on the front porch of the bank man's house where beans grew wild in the front yard, looking out into the wherever the other one might be. Her sadness was magic and we never got her back.

We went off to university, each to our own liking. Paid for it all with hard earned scholarships won after years of her telling us how a lady can do what she sees fit in this world if she wants it enough. One of us a musician, one an architect, and one a mother just like her with dreams and farm to tend.

We gather when we can and talk about the times gone away, what might have been, and the wonder of what turned out to be. In our dreams, we go back to our burned farmhouse, all black inside. We hear her humming, louder, but farther away. We look for her, but she isn't there. So we sit cross-legged in the empty hallway, and wait, moving our hands through the smoke like shelling beans, remembering the three of us, little and dumbfounded, somewhere between what was and what would be, ushered into the grass and grit without a chance to salvage anything.

HUNGRY

She takes them to the park to preoccupy them with swing sets and jungle gyms. Tells them, when they ask, "You ate already," like they're tiny Alzheimer's patients who can be fooled with reassuring words and misdirection. She tried not to go on food stamps, but pride gives way easy to a child's aching stomach. She remembers the jabs about government cheese and welfare babies she heard as a child. But those words didn't apply to her then, well dressed and fed and unaware of what it meant to be a scavenger.

She gets enough on her little plastic card to last them the most of the month, but those last few days feel pretty thin. She works. She manages to keep the lights on and the rent paid most months but sometimes they spend a few days in the dark. She tells them they're on adventure—camping in the living room. Candles and ghost stories. Cold beans from the can.

A few times she's had to barter with the landlord—cleaning his house, mowing the lawn. Once when the whole of the rent went to fixing up her busted Buick, she gave in a bit more than she wanted. She would have cried about it, but there was no need to waste tears on necessity.

When she did cry, she knew how to hide it, how to turn her face and wipe the tears, smile like those mothers who come through her checkout line buying fresh fruit and good meat and deli slices of cheese to fill whole wheat, all natural, bakery fresh bread for their well dressed children's lunch sacks.

The same women look at her when she drops her kids off at school. The look says she doesn't care because her children are dressed in Goodwill clothing and the pre-sliced cheese in their store brand bread sandwiches came wrapped in plastic. She knows her kids look, at best, well worn. They aren't bathed every night because water and heat cost money. She hates the looks from those mothers accusing her, assuming she doesn't love her kids as much as they do, when perhaps, perhaps, she knows how to love them more. Knows how desperate love can be when there is a chance it could be taken away.

She knows to fear that knock on the door. The clipboard and the questions. They don't know what they're asking. They don't understand the gravity of her answers. She's making up for her past, even now. She's a good mother. She takes them to the library where she can let them pick whatever they want. She can't afford to own the pages, but she can give them the words. Stories of adventure and triumph, castles and fairies and happy ever after. It breaks her heart to know that one day the world will show them all that these fairytales are not.

When her hours are cut at work and her car has left them stranded and in need of more repair than it's worth, she still tries to make do as best she can. She walks them to the school bus stop and then continues on foot to her job or goes into town to panhandle.

The power goes out and does not come back on. The landlord has had his fill and posts the little pink slip on her door. She makes the most of their last days in a private living space. She reads them books by candlelight and tells wild stories of peril and triumph and when her time is up she packs their little bags with what's left to cart away. She takes them from shelter to shelter. She's tired of staying awake most of the night, holding onto them as they sleep.

She takes them to DSS like turning in a litter of kittens. Perhaps some nice family might take them in. Buy them new clothes, tuck them in—warm and safe into a bed dressed with new sheets and a downy comforter. They sit outside the government building with her arms wrapped around them, the air in her chest ripped up and as cold as the January around them, cutting her throat on the way in and out.

"What are we doing, Mommy?" the older one asks, and the sound of the little voice cracks what's left of her.

In the end, she can't do it. Better that she cut out her heart for that nice rich family to fry up in a fancy meal. Instead, she pulls their secondhand coats tight around them and walks away from the government building. Two blocks down, she pulls open the heavy wooden doors of the church she knew as a child, walks them all the way to the toes of Jesus, and shows them how to kneel down and pray.

THE INTERRING OF WHAT REMAINS

Tell me about that night," the woman with the clipboard and the name-badge, and no way to understand, said to her.

The room they met in never warmed up like it should, even though the heater blew the entire hour. All noise and no effect.

"That year, the clock in the hall stopped ticking," the girl said. "No one set it and time stood still."

"It just seemed that way," the useless woman said. "Time can't stand still."

"It's standing still right now."

The air had been soft and cool, but whether it was the burst of spring or the relief of fall, the girl didn't know. She couldn't recall if the green was coming or going. Just that it was one of those easy nights with the windows open and the covers thrown down around the ankles of the bed. The moon rose high and fat and the white, cotton curtains billowed in and out like breath.

Had she simply wandered, in the late night, down the steps to the kitchen or had someone called her—

whispering her name up the empty stairwell? The patter of her tiptoeing crunched against the floorboards like breaking ice.

Now that she thought about it, had it been green at all? Was she just imagining that color, hadn't it all been red except for the snow? Or was that just the thick, sweet magnolia petals and not snowflakes at all—the red simply the hand grenade bulbs falling from the twist of the tree.

Somewhere in the darkness of the house, the girl had heard someone crying. Of that she was sure. Slipping into the shadows she peeked over the sofa into a room full of swirl and sadness. In the corner, she saw her sister—half lit by fat moonlight sticking in her hair— hair like unstoppable fire.

Much as she wanted them not to, the memories clung to the girl's clothes, stuck to her skin, like the smell of the shore or campfire—something that time had trouble wearing away. But like a dream, the patterns of logic were wrong, incoherent around the edges.

Had she been seven? Probably ten, that would make more sense. Or maybe fourteen. Maybe none of those. Was it before the night in the boathouse? Or after, during the summer, somewhere amid those months that it rained every day, so that water flowed down the hallway—up to her ankles for weeks.

"Why do think there was water in the hallway?" the woman with the name badge questioned and slipped her white jacket off her shoulders.

"My feet were wet," the girl said, lifting them off the floor, just in case the water flowed still. "Everything was wet. The tide came in under the door frame."

"What door frame?" the woman asked and searched her paperwork for some prior information.

The girl shrugged like she had been over that a thousand times. She looked at the name-badge the woman wore, but none of the words behind the plastic made any sense.

"To the boathouse," the girl said.

"You didn't have a boathouse."

"I know that."

Crouching behind the couch, peeping up like she was spying a ghost, the girl had watched. Saw her mother slip to the table in the dining room, wrap up the linen cloth—stark white like the moon, but black in places—or red.

The girl had not seen her sister in months, but knew that she had been somewhere in the house. Could hear her talking in the rafters when the leaves had begun to die, when the ground was finally frozen solid. When everything whispered against the glass in the windows—when no one in the house spoke.

"Just go," the girl's father ordered to a stranger in the doorway. The stranger lifted a bundle to his shoulder. Something small, wrapped tight in a blanket. It wiggled and he held it closer as he left. Snow drifted in when he opened the door. Or was it just the chill of the room drifting out?

Her mother pressed by the father and turned her face from him. She thrust the table linen at the sister, who stumbled to her feet and went out into the yard. When the parents had gone upstairs the girl followed her sister into the garden—watched as she dug, deep down below the lilies. Maybe it had been spring or maybe the lilies were dead, these were the places the girl couldn't straighten out in her mind. She couldn't find the color cues that would make it all make sense. She only remembered red.

Her sister placed the cloth inside the hole underneath the flowers.

"Where do you think your sister was?" the unstoppable woman went on.

"In the dark above me."

"In the house?" The woman wrote once more in her notes.

The plastic chair the girl sat in made everything uncomfortable. The art on the walls was done by mental patients. The useless heater never stopped running.

"Maybe. Maybe in the magnolia outside my bedroom window."

"That's not where she was," the woman said and shook her head at the girl.

"I know."

Outside, there had been ice on the daylilies. She knew it wasn't cold, but that's the way she saw it. For weeks before, she had heard her sister's voice in the gnarled tree outside her bedroom window. Her sister was talking about things that the girl could scarcely remember.

"Come on, silly," her sister whispered from the branches, "you remember. You cracked the ground when you came in."

"I don't remember."

"The water was running in the sink," her sister said, "fog clouds were all around the dock. We were in the boat."

"We didn't have a boat," the girl had said, pulling the bed covers up over her like a tomb.

"I know that," her sister's voice said—clear even through the thick of the blankets.

"I don't understand."

"Yes you do," her sister pleaded the truth to the

surface. "You parted the pink sail and there we were in the porcelain belly, you remember our boat, set sail across the tiled sea."

"Where we used to search for pirates?" the girl asked peeking out.

Her sister's tears watered the ground, streaking the windowpane, and the girl nodded. Tulips and poppies sprang up beneath the window, grew high as the lowest magnolia branch and then wilted away into nothing.

When the girl took a breath, the air was cold and when she breathed out—fog.

"Do you know what was in the blanket?" The woman wouldn't stop asking that question.

The girl shook her head.

"I think you do," the woman prodded.

"Then why do you keep asking?" The girl looked the woman in the eye.

The woman looked away.

The morning after, at the kitchen table, over orange juice and pancakes, the girl had watched the mother and father smile at her sister as if she had never been hidden away, as if her eyes were not weary with tears, as if she weren't disappearing slowly, slowly before them. The next summer, it rained. A thunderstorm in the stairwell, black clouds floated down the hall. The girl never saw her sister smile again.

Years later, after winter stopped ending, they still spoke of her sister at the snowy dinner table, brushed icicles from their eyebrows and smiled—smiled as if her sorrow never rose up and broke the moon.

STEPPING OUT IN FRONT OF THE TRAIN

Every year I buy poppy seeds that I know I won't plant."

There's nowhere to grow them in my tiny apartment in the city. The packets fill a shoebox in the back of my dresser drawer.

"One day I'll plant them and cover my half of the world."

"Charlotte," my therapist says to this, "after this long, do you really think they would grow?"

"That's not the point."

"Do you know what the point is?" She slides in her seat and the silk of her skirt kisses across the leather cushion like water rolling off a rock.

"Does there have to be one?" I ask.

"There usually is."

My therapist talks to me in a slow, soothing voice. It irritates me, but I think she knows that.

"Charlotte," she coos, "I want you to close your eyes. I want you to see that Sunday again. I want you to feel the breeze on your skin, to hear the tiny tinkle of the chimes." She waves her hands around in the air. "I want you to remember what really happened. Listen to the chimes, Charlotte, hear the music flowing over you."

I stare straight ahead.

"I hear the train. I don't hear any music. I just hear the train."

Her hands fall to her thighs.

"I can't help you, Charlotte, as long as you insist on only hearing the train."

"It's so loud," I whisper. "How can I hear anything else."

That Sunday, I had waited for my boyfriend on the front porch of our rickety, white house. My mother came out—handed me my Bible.

"Charlotte," she said, "you'll need this for church."

Behind her head, silver wind chimes rang out with the hot breeze. She spoke something more, but the wind picked up and drowned her out with music. Sun spiked off the silver chimes, glinting in my eyes when she moved away.

"Did you hear me, Charlotte?" She stopped before going back inside—planted her hands on her hips, apron dusty with flour from the morning biscuits.

"Yes, Ma'am."

My mother never left our house anymore. Couldn't make it down the front steps without gagging for air and reaching out for something to take hold of.

In the distance Robbie crossed the railroad tracks next to our house and swaggered up the dirt drive. Robbie was twenty, wore tight jeans on Sunday and my stepfather loathed the sight of him. Wanted to put him in jail for touching me, but he didn't have the nerve.

"You ready, Charlotte?" Robbie held his hand out to me, eyes like rich earth peering from behind wild, dirty blonde hair.

I put the Bible on the porch swing and took Robbie's

hand. My stepfather came out, walking loudly in his shiny church shoes.

"Morning, son," he said to Robbie. Nothing to me.

"Reverend Mills." Robbie nodded back at him, both of them tall, lean, one of them mean.

The two stood their ground on either side of me— both churning like the place where the river meets the ocean. I tugged Robbie's hand and we left my stepfather standing on the porch. I turned back to see him pick up my Bible and hold it to his cheek.

My fancy New York City therapist tells me I make bad choices. She says they stem from my feelings about my stepfather and the "train incident."

No kidding.

She looks at me across her big mahogany desk and taps her pencil to its top. Closing her eyes, she says, "Charlotte, you need to face facts and relive that day in order to get it out of your system."

"What are you talking about?" I ask her. "I relive it every day."

Bright blue Sunday morning—high summer and hot— Robbie Doyle and I skipped worship and laid out in the warm green grass behind the sanctuary, behind my stepfather in the pulpit. A stone angel stood at the top of my head, bright orange poppies licking up the side of her rock dress, a crack in her wing running like a spider vein across the feathers.

"Charlotte," Robbie pleaded although there was no need, "can I?" His hands hovered over me.

Silence was a yes. I turned my head to the side, reached for the poppies beneath the angel's feet.

"Charlotte," he whispered my name over and over, "Charlotte."

I plucked the grass at my side, blade by blade, as he moved in and out. He rolled over in the grass beside me when he was done. I didn't care that we were in back of the church, wide open to anyone who would look. I did it on purpose because I hated the man on the other side of the red brick wall.

I hated him.

Choir voices carried on the wind—and He walks with me and He talks with me. He tells me I am his own.

I sleep soundly in the city like I never did back home. The crickets and cicadas were like little winged monsters in the night. Growing louder and louder as the years passed. Here, hundreds of miles away, the honking horns are like Heaven's chorus. Noisy bliss to drive out the sound of the train.

"What did your therapist say today?" the man in bed beside me asks in the darkness.

"Same thing she always says."

"Maybe you should listen to her," he says and rolls away from me.

"How can I listen to her when wind chimes ring out from her mouth?'

"Charlotte, don't be melodramatic. No one in the city has wind chimes."

Tomorrow I'll ask him to leave, just like the others.

"Why weren't you in church today?" My stepfather asked as he unzipped his pants.

My mother was in the kitchen making dinner. Humming to herself, covering up the silence.

"I was outside screwing Robbie Doyle," I said. Honesty, when there is nothing else. "Are you jealous, Father?"

"Don't call me that." My stepfather pushed me down on my knees in front of him.

I did what he wanted.

He zipped his pants and adjusted his belt. I flinched. I hated myself for flinching.

"Get out," he said. "I've got work to do."

I went out in the kitchen and sat at the table. My mother stopped humming and held tight to the lip of the sink as if the earth was quaking under her feet. I thumbed through the cookbook on the table. My hands steady, my mind like a whirling dervish, spinning a hole in the world around me.

The next Sunday I sat in the front row. Robbie sat beside me and I didn't take my eyes off my stepfather at all. That made him nervous and angry and when the service was over and he was standing down front, waiting to bring people to Jesus, I went to him and knelt at his feet.

"Get up, Charlotte," he hissed at me, "go home."

"Forgive me, Father," I said to someone more holy than he, "for we have sinned."

"Charlotte," he must have thought he was whispering, but he was yelling at me. "Get up and get out of here."

"Ask to be forgiven," I said to him. "Ask."

"Shut up, Charlotte."

I knew there were eyes on us. I knew I had won. He grabbed me up by the hair and dragged me out of the church and then like a madman, someone possessed, he lugged me three blocks to the railroad tracks. He panted like an old mule, but kept going past our house and up the hill to the railroad crossing.

He flung me down in the dirt near the edge of the tracks. He never looked back at the crowd catching up to us.

"The Bible says whores should perish, fornicators be damned to Hell by the wrath of an angry God."

I wasn't sure the Bible said those things at all, but it

didn't really matter. Because that's when I heard it. A low rumble in the distance. The train.

His small congregation had made its way down to the tracks. Someone yelled for the women and children to stay back. Behind my father, several men crept up like stalking tigers.

My mother came spilling down the porch steps, racing to the tracks. She tried to push forward though the crowd, but someone held her back. Her fists flailed in the air like a two-year-old in a tantrum. My stepfather looked only at me, his face sweaty and red. He grabbed me by the hair and dragged me closer to the tracks. The ground shook with the weight of the train bearing down. I looked up at him through the veil of my twisted hair. His eyes were wet with rage, or sorrow — both or neither.

The train thundered forward and when it neared us, whistle piercing the air, my stepfather let loose of me and stepped out in front of it. Men shouted out — mouths agape, no sound — women turned their heads and covered children's eyes. But me, I stepped back and looked straight ahead as the train hit my stepfather in the chest and whisked him away.

As the last train car passed us by, wheels squealing in effort to stop, my mother's wind chimes sounded in their wake. She was standing out in the crowd, out in the street, with her hand raised up. I'm not sure if it was lifted in shock, as if she were trying to cover the sight, or if she was waving goodbye.

Underground at Broadway, I stand in line for the express as it thunders forward. I skipped my therapist appointment today. I do that sometimes. It doesn't seem to make any difference. I'm staring off into space the way people do when they wait, but in my mind I step out in front of the train, arms outstretched, smiling.

Nobody Next Door

He lived in the apartment next door to her. Lanky and out of sorts, he was sometimes mistaken for drunk, but actually it was more the result of acid or maybe mushrooms if he felt like doing it the natural way. She liked the looks of him. His auburn goatee and darker disheveled hair gave him the appearance of one of those gunslingers on Wild West movie remakes. Except that he was much too tall to look right on film and, of course, his usual garb of jeans and T-shirts didn't befit an Earp or a James or any one of a dozen other nicknamed men from a time long ago.

On occasion she had encountered him in the elevator, dressed as a vampire on his way to some role-playing meet-up, the details of which they would talk about on the seven-floor descent in a one-sided conversation where he attempted to explain the concept of make-believe and live-action role play and she nodded while trying to gain some perspective of where each of the players stood in the room and whether they were actually interacting with each other like in a stage play or if it was all on the computer and merely in each of their minds. But then again, he was dressed as a vampire and leaving the building, so she supposed it must be real.

He was far less boisterous than the fellows with whom he spent his time and he, unlike the rest of them, never made rudely suggestive comments about her pencil skirts and tights. She supposed the others were just making fun of her and she was divided in thought on which of their offenses was worse.

She was mostly mistaken for a school teacher although she wasn't sure why. She had given up explaining what it was that she did. It seemed not to hold any interest once she began explaining statistical analysis and data configuration so she left off correcting people when they made false assumptions. She was altogether unsure what he did for a living and really there were several things that he did to pay the bills, most of which paid under the table so he had far less paperwork to keep up with than most people did come tax season. Most days he was home by the time she got off the subway and up the elevator. Sometimes, she would linger outside his door listening to what sounded like Japanese combat set to techno music. Although she could hear better through their shared interior wall, she sometimes waited outside her door in the hope that he might come out. On the rare occasion that he did, he smiled as if he had been hoping to see her too and whether he fell for her attempts to appear to be fumbling for her keys, she didn't know.

"The average person will accidently swallow thirty spiders over the course of their life," he said one day as they waited on the sixth floor for someone else to get into the elevator.

She figured herself pretty average and this was new and disturbing information.

"What about you?" she asked once they were headed down again.

"I figure I'm up to about twenty-eight by now," he said and tugged on his black cloak, arranging himself and nodding to the old lady who made everyone chocolate peanut butter balls for Christmas.

"Planning to spread the last two out?" she asked when the door opened.

"If all goes well," he said to her and just before the three of them stepped out of the elevator he put his hand on the old lady's shoulder. "Thanks for the nut balls, Mrs. Watson."

She wondered if Mrs. Watson had already swallowed her allotted amount of spiders. If perhaps, unbeknownst to her, this was the last time Mrs. Watson would ride down the elevator and step out into the nicotine-colored lobby of the fifth oldest apartment building in the city. The thought of spiders in an hourglass came to mind and she wondered if one could prolong their life if they made themselves extraordinary enough to warrant a higher number of accidental ingestions. She also thought of sleeping with her mouth taped shut.

The only person who ever knocked on her door was the kid from the sushi delivery place and when she heard the rapping it took a moment for her to remember whether she had placed an order. Upon opening it and seeing her neighbor and not the sushi kid, she was very aware that she was more appropriately dressed for dragon rolls than for this unprecedented visit from the man next door.

"I can see from your face you thought I was the sushi kid," he said.

She stepped back to let him in and then wondered if the gesture would go unaccepted, making the space between them less an invitation and more an awkward realization. He stepped inside.

"So," she said and stood watching him decide where to sit, if to sit, where to stand, if to stand, "were you the sushi kid, what would you have brought?"

"Most anything with tuna," he said, pleasing her that they were in sync in this nonsensical conversation.

He sat on the left end of the couch. She sat on the right. They said nothing for quite some time and then after a while he got up and began walking around her apartment inspecting things like he was in an oddities shop.

"Is that a hamster?" he asked about the only other thing that lived in her sparsely appointed apartment.

"It's a rat," she said and came to stand just slightly behind him.

He laughed and shook his head.

"I hate rats," he said, turning toward her. "Who has a rat as a pet?"

He reached out toward her and tucked a piece of her hair behind her ear. He was at least a foot taller than she and it made her feel small and safe, yet afraid that if he fell she would not be able to catch him.

"Do you have any more Vicodin?" he asked, lowering his gaze. "From when you had that root canal?"

She did. She had only taken one of them and it had made her so sick that she had called out of work the next day. She went to the bathroom to retrieve the bottle that she had kept because it seemed too important to throw away. His eyes were grayer than usual and apologetic as he reached out for it. She wasn't used to people listening to her when she chattered on about things like root canals, sushi delivery boys, and left-over medicine.

"Are you ok?" she asked as she pressed the bottle into the cool sweat of his palm.

"From time to time," he answered and tucked the piece of her hair back again from where it had come undone.

Several weeks went by that she did not see him and her increasing anxiety over the matter led her to wiggle his doorknob. Finding it unlocked, she sneaked inside the apartment and found him sitting in a recliner with his leg in a brace, staring at the Japanese fighting game she had heard so many times, stuck on a demo that repeated every few minutes. She sat on the couch for quite a long time hoping that he would notice her there. He did not, but instead closed his eyes and after a while fell asleep. His head dipped slightly and his lips parted. She went and knelt beside the recliner. She wanted to put her mouth to his, but instead she put her head on his chest and listened to his heart. It beat loud and mechanical-sounding and perfectly timed like the clock that ticked over her cubical all day at work.

Eventually he stirred and she jerked up and away from him. Their eyes met and although it was out of the ordinary for her to be in his apartment, kneeling down beside him in his living room, he did not seem unpleased to see her. He cleared his throat and resumed the combat game. She moved back to the couch and watched a small brown spider on the corner of the entertainment center wander around like it was looking for a way down.

In the weeks that followed he made no indication when he saw her that anything out of the ordinary had transpired and she wondered if perhaps he did not remember it. She didn't mention the leg brace or its absence now in case it might stir some memory to which she couldn't predict the implication.

They shared their usual conversations and when they met in the hallway at 6:30pm on a Tuesday night, she anticipated further details about the state of play at the vampire gathering. Truth be told, she had no place in particular to go, she simply knew that he would leave at that precise time on that day to meet up with his friends and she would have him to herself for seven floors. Assuming, that is, that no one else in the building had any need to ride the elevator.

He smiled when he saw her and she smiled back. The skin at his temple glistened like everyone's seemed to in August when the corridors and confined spaces were sticky with summer in a place that had no air conditioning.

"So," she inquired of him, bringing up an earlier conversation. "Are you going to accept the position as high vampire controller or are you thinking of running things from behind the scenes?"

He laughed and she knew it was because she was getting the terminology wrong. However, it wasn't the sort of laugh that made her feel as though she had said something stupid, but rather a chuckle of endearment that made her feel close to him.

"I haven't quite decided," he said and then stepped back from her like there had been a jolt on the elevator that she had not felt.

He drew in a sharp breath and went down on one knee. She wondered only briefly if he were play-acting something for her, but his eyes caught hers and she knew he was not. This happened on the sixth floor and by the fourth she was crouched down beside him shouting his name at him, realizing that she had never said his name in anything more that a whisper to herself. When they reached the bottom floor she had already pulled out her phone and was calling for help.

The door opened and there were people in the lobby, but because they were all taken aback at the scene before them and unaware of what to do, they all remained frozen in place and she perceived them like they were a painting in an art gallery. The door closed back after a few moments and she had him all to herself one more time.

She sat on her knees in the back triangle created by his supine body where he lay diagonally across the elevator floor. She leaned again to listen to the clock tick in his chest. His breathing was labored and shallow and she couldn't hear anything over the rapid rise and fall of the cage surrounding his heart. His eyes flickered from her to the ceiling to her again and stayed there. He reached out for her hand and she wound her fingers around his. He moved his lips to speak to her, but she couldn't hear his voice—low and trapped somewhere too far down to get out. She pressed her other hand to his forehead and then buried her fingers in his hair. She leaned in, trying to hear him and once she was close enough to feel his breath on her cheek she heard a few words and then he didn't say anything else. She sat up a bit and he lifted his other hand to touch her hair.

The elevator jerked into motion, headed up. It stopped on the third floor and when the door opened onto the widower whose wife's funeral they had both attended earlier that year, she very calmly asked him to please send them back down.

When they reached the lobby again, the door opened onto paramedics and the like and she was hustled further to the back of the elevator. As they took him out, someone mistook her for his girlfriend and asked if she would go back to their apartment and get whatever medical records or such that a doctor would want to see and that perhaps she should begin to call his family and meet them at the hospital.

"What's his name?" they yelled to her. "What's his name?"

"Andrew," she said.

"Andy," they called out to him, "hang in there, buddy."

She imagined they were doing that for her benefit as they didn't hold much hope in their faces. She thought he probably went by Andy, but that was not how he had introduced himself to her. She rode the elevator back up to the seventh floor although she wasn't sure what she should do. She wiggled the doorknob on his apartment but it was locked. She knocked; perhaps one of his friends would come to the door. She supposed she could find the Super and see if he would let her in, seeing as how it was an emergency.

Instead she went inside her own place where she had a lasagna in the oven because she hadn't planned on going anywhere once the elevator got to the lobby anyway. She had meant to check her mail and maybe exit the building going in the opposite direction of him as if she were running an errand, then cut the block and go back home. Once inside, she pressed her ear to the wall they shared. She could hear a faint music, his game left on, repeating its opening sequence, expecting for someone to press play.

She turned off the oven and went back into the hall. She sat on the floor between the two apartments and watched the elevator lights. After a very long while a man, some fifty-plus years old, stepped off the elevator and went to Andrew's door. She scrambled to stand up, her legs tingling from being in a fixed position for too long.

"Are you here about Andrew?" she asked.

"Who are you?" the man asked in a panic that gave him away as Andrew's father.

She felt unnecessary.

"No one," she said and went back into her apartment.

She had gone that first day to the hospital, but as she was not family and did not have the nerve to lie, she was not permitted in. She inquired daily on the phone as to what room he was in, in hopes that the number would come back different and he would no longer be in the ICU. Eventually the receptionist learned to recognize her voice and would just say, "Nothing has changed, sweetie. Why don't you call his family and talk to them?" She continued her phone inquiry until the receptionist asked her to please stop, causing her to feel foolish and she did not call back.

She figured it for the best. Perhaps she would have called one last time and been told that there was no patient by that name in the hospital and she would have to imagine spiders in the bottom of an hourglass and that Japanese combat game stuck forever on demo.

She moved to an apartment on the fifth floor to avoid seeing someone come for his things or to notice a new tenant. This way, she would not have to know and hopefully, she could encounter him in the future, in the elevator on his way out to the vampire game, and when she imagined his hourglass there would be at least one spider clinging to the top, too fat to fall through.

THE DOWNSIDE OF REDEMPTION

I 've reached that point in my life where it's become absolutely necessary to become a hooker."

"Excuse me?" Paul, my husband who hates the restaurant we're in, asks from behind the *Daily Times*.

The waitress clears her throat.

"They have such perfect timing, don't they," Paul says, more to her than to me.

"A hooker, Paul," I say to him, and to the waitress I nod at my cup, indicating I'll take more coffee.

"I wasn't aware," he says, folding down but not closing the paper, "that there was such a thing."

"You're not aware of hookers?" I ask.

"No, June," he says and sighs, "I wasn't aware that there was a time when it became absolutely necessary to become one."

"I'm not talking about being a whore," I interject, "I'd only be in it for the money. I don't imagine the sex would be very good."

Paul opens his mouth to comment, but my brother, Michael, joins us at the table before Paul can get the words past his lips.

"So what's up," Michael asks, raising his hand at the waitress—signaling for a drink.

"Your sister is a whore," Paul states and flips the paper barricade back in front of his face.

"What?" Michael asks toward the paper, hand frozen in the air.

"A hooker," I say to correct Paul.

"What?" Michael raises his voice, looking back and forth from me to Paul's paper—hand still in the air.

"I'm not one yet," I say to calm him down.

"Yet." Comes the sarcastic repeat from behind the news. Michael lowers his hand.

"What the hell is this about?" he asks.

The waitress returns now with our drinks. Coffee for me and a whiskey sour for Michael that he didn't even have to order. Michael winks at her and she blushes ever so slightly.

"Anyway, June," Paul says, finished with the paper now and folding it annoyingly back into shape, "don't you think it's a little cold to become a hooker. It's the dead of winter, for crying out loud."

"Is this a joke?" Michael asks, lifting, but not sipping from his drink.

"This is what you're worried about?" I ask pointedly, "The weather?"

"Well, for Christ's sake, June, I don't think you're serious."

"So this is a joke?" Michael asks again, sipping now, then setting the drink back on its coaster.

"Of course it's a joke, moron," Paul aims his words at Michael, "what rational person would become a hooker?"

"Dude," Michael says, "I'm not a moron."

"Oh really," Paul says. "Can you tell me one thing that you know about current events that doesn't have to do with boob jobs and sports scores."

Michaels looks around as if to find a comeback on the walls.

"That's what I thought," Paul says and reaches for his wallet, "I'll be paying the bill now, Michael, so if there's anything else you want to mooch, now would be the time to inconspicuously place your order."

Michael gives Paul the finger and opens up one of the menus on the table. Paul huffs, but waits to pull out his wallet until Michael places his order.

"Give me the ten piece wings," he says to the waitress who has been hovering since Michael showed up, "make 'em hot and also the Pounder Burger with Swiss and another one of these." He finishes by pointing at his drink.

The waitress leaves before I can ask her to get me a whiskey sour as well.

"I'm going back to work, June," Paul states as he stands. "I really do hate this place."

Paul drops some money on the table, not waiting for the check, tucks his paper under his arm and wipes his coat as if to clean away even the smells of this low class establishment he has come to out of obligation.

Michael moves around to take Paul's empty chair.

"What's up with him?" Michael asks. "And what's this about you being a hooker?"

"I don't know," I say. "I'm just spitballing."

"Do you think this would attract men?" I ask, holding up a leather skirt, or some sort of scarf that's intent is to be a skirt.

The salesclerk nods approval and I tuck the article under my arm.

I stroll around the display of half shirts and backless tops looking for something to match.

"It's a little cold for that," an old lady says from behind a distant rack. "It's the dead of winter, you know."

I smile and say, "I know." And wonder what this old lady is doing in a store called Sweet Tarts.

I select a top and make my purchase.

I think this may be a bad idea.

But I'm all out of ideas and this seems like the next logical step. I don't need the money, but I need the distraction— so a part time job seems appealing. I applied for salesclerk jobs which I didn't get because, get this, I didn't have any experience. It's not brain surgery I told them, but that didn't seem to help. I applied for waitressing positions, again it was, "Sorry, but we're looking for a girl with experience."

Daycare: "Sorry, but it really does help if you've had experience."

Secretarial jobs: "Oh, you've never worked in an office? We're looking for someone with experience."

So it's come down to hooker, because, dammit, I'm experienced.

And it's good, you know, because I can set my own hours and wages. There's no uniform and no boss. I've had enough of being "Paul's Wife" and living Paul's life. And secretly I know I'm not serious. I won't really put this outfit on and walk the streets of small town suburbia asking people's husbands and fathers if they're looking for a date.

But I like to think that I would. That I could put on some short little number and walk out in the cold with no one to back me up but me. I like to imagine that I could withstand the wind, that I could brave the blizzarding cold. That I wouldn't give up and go in.

Back at home in my regular t-shirt and gray sweats, I get a phone call from Paul stating that he's going to be late and not to bother with dinner. I wish he would "bother" to call me before I had already spent an hour cooking.

So I Tupper-ware everything into the fridge, noticing the other containers of missed dinners that litter the shelves, the side compartments, every available space. I've given up on cleaning them out. I'm waiting for the damn thing to be full, like it's going to prove a point to someone other than myself.

It's impossible to prove a point to someone who doesn't even care that you've got one to prove.

I wash the dishes and wipe off the counters. I put spices back on the shelf and toss scraps into the trash. And all the while I'm thinking about that skirt and that tight little shirt. So I think—what the hell. I'll just put it on. Wear it around the house. It will be funny. Not pathetic in any way.

I go into the bedroom and approach the shopping bag like it's a bomb. I slide my hand into the plastic without looking and retrieve the shirt. I'm relieved. The shirt is the lesser of the two evils. The shirt will just make me a hussy. It's the skirt that really makes the whore.

I remove my upper clothing, bra and all, and squeeze into the hot pink, sequined half top. My breasts spill over the top just like any good hussy's would. I want to look in the mirror, but I can't bring myself to do it just yet.

I sneak my hand back into the bag and carefully pull out the tiny piece of snakeskin printed leather. I inch out of the gray sweats and into something much less comfortable.

What would Paul think if he saw me in this? He'd roll his eyes.

"Take that ridiculous thing off, June," I voice his words out loud.

I don't take it off.

There. Now with new courage I realize I need shoes. How could I have forgotten the shoes?

"Maybe I have something that will do," I say aloud

and begin to rummage through the closet. And there, way in the back, on Paul's side, I find a pair of black spiked heels.

"Ah ha," I say and sit on the floor to put them on. They're a bit too tight. And I wonder why these too little, unfamiliar shoes are in my closet, way at the back on Paul's side.

So, I'm ready. The look is complete.

And I think—I should have something to drink. A woman wearing clothes like this must need a drink.

So here we are, me and my outfit, sipping our fifth whiskey sour and thinking that maybe we should go for a drive. Just tool around town. See who's out and about. Surely my outfit and I can make a buck or two, show Paul that we can fend for ourselves.

So we walk out the front door, drink in hand and head for the Grand Am. One of us drops the drink on the lawn, but we let it slide. We back into the mailbox on the way out of the driveway, but that's ok, we hated that mailbox anyway.

On the way into town we pass Mrs. Cutler and wave at her, but she just shakes her snow shovel at us and yells something about the wrong side of the street. We decide to park the car in the City Hall parking lot, but somehow it gets parked on the front lawn instead. We figure it's late and all those windbags are gone home anyway, so we just leave it there.

My outfit and I decide to go over to Bud and Joe's. It's the only bar in town except for the two seater at the Lion's Den, but that's not the same thing. We get in there and adjust our eyes to the low light and heavy smoke haze. Now certainly there will be someone in here who would like to buy a lady and her skimpy outfit a drink.

We take a seat at the bar and wait. We've never been

in this place and now we see why. What a hole. There are three or four wobbly tables scattered around the room. Each table is already littered with beer bottles, dirty glasses of melting ice, and the elbows of drunks propping themselves up to continue their conversations. Cigarette butts and bits of food cover the floor. One cigarette is still burning.

There seems to be about five of the same guy at one table or it may be that they are all wearing a similar uniform. Who knows?

"You seem a bit out of sorts, ma'am," the lone man at the end of the bar says to us.

"We're fine," I say and he looks past my shoulder, glancing around.

"We?" he asks.

"That's right," I answer. "Look, are you going to buy us a drink or not?"

We keep slipping off the barstool.

"You bring a friend?" he asks and he seems like he's intrigued by this.

"No," I answer, and burp, "did you?"

"You want me to get one?" he asks. "Because if that's what you're looking for..."

He doesn't finish the sentence, but it's one of those that doesn't need finishing.

"You gotta pay us, you know," I say, "and where's our drink."

"I'm going to have to see who 'we' is first," this man who really can't afford to be all that picky is saying, but I've stopped listening to him.

Obviously he's not going to buy us a drink so we're moving on.

"Oh, god," a familiar man's voice says and for a second I think it's Paul. But it isn't, it's Michael.

"June?" he asks, positioning himself in front of me to

keep the prying eyes off, "what in God's name are you doing?"

"Michael?" I ask and fall off the barstool.

I stand, and one ankle buckles over in the too tight, not mine, black spiked heels.

Michael holds me steady.

"Hey," I say to him, "what are you doing in here? This place is a hole."

And then I realize that I'm in a bar, dressed like a hooker, and things get this clarity that I wish they didn't have.

"Did you bring a coat?" Michael is asking. "It's freezing out, June. Why are you dressed like this?"

"I've become a hooker," I say and hang my head.

People are looking at us and I'm not sure what to do about that.

"You're not a hooker, June," Michael says, takes off his coat and hands it to me.

"I might as well be," I say, struggling to get my arms into the sleeves.

"Don't be ridiculous."

"I think it's a little late for that," I reply.

"Let's go home, June." Michael leads me out into the cold. "You'll sober up, put your real clothes back on and this will just be some crazy thing you did one night."

"That we keep to ourselves?"

"Absolutely," Michael says.

I nod and think how I'll refer back to all this in my mind as the night I showed Paul what I was made of—not that he'll ever know. It takes a lot of courage to do something this stupid. Maybe the night I showed myself is more like it. I start to feel better even as my head starts to pound. Maybe I've been too hard on myself, too hard on Paul. Maybe these black heels fit me after all.

Michael is asking me where I parked and looking

around for the car. He finally gets his own keys when I'm not able to offer an answer. He's telling me that we'll just take his car and that he'll sleep at my place and get my car later, but I'm not hearing any of that. All I hear is a another familiar voice and a woman laughing.

As Michael helps me into his car, placing his hand on my head as he ducks me in, like I'm a criminal, I see Paul and some woman who probably looks good in black spiked heels and it finally hits me just how cold it is.

ROTTEN ORANGES

Nights, my sister and I lie out in the yard and listen for rotten oranges to thump to the ground. Mornings, we beat even the birdsong to the river's edge to toss those oranges in. Their soft, spotted bodies plunk through the thick, Florida river on their way to the bottom. The fruit makes ripples in the water that go out in circles too many to count.

My sister always throws one close to the bank so that later she can come back to look at it, stuck down in the gunk.

"That one is me," she says today.

I raise my orange to toss it in next to hers and she slaps it from my hand.

"Yours can't be with mine," she says.

When I wail a "why not" she turns away from me so that she thinks I don't see her start to cry. When I try to touch her hair she jerks away.

We set to heaving more rotting fruit into the water and then later when my sister decides enough oranges have gone in, we race the heat to the end of the boat dock where we sit in the wee shade of the lifted Mako Angler and wait for the fisherman to come around in their little boats with their red coolers in the back and their bright blue life jackets tossed to the front. I like to trace my finger over the raised red letters on the side of my father's boat.

Mako Angler.

My father has told me that a Mako is a shark and that an Angler is a fisherman. Sometimes I dream about my father in his Mako, hunting down sharks. Sometimes the sharks flip the little boat over and my father is gobbled up.

My sister and I wave at the summer people as they pass. Most of the time they wave back with the lift of a beer held firm in their hands. Sometimes the bikini people come by on their ski boats. They laugh over their loud music, yelling out to each other and to us when we wave.

We will sit there for hours, watching and waiting for something to happen. Nothing usually does. My sister likes to sun herself on the dock. She pushes up the legs of her shorts so that she doesn't get a tan line she says. She rests back on her palms, one leg out straight and the other bent up so that she looks like a movie star to me, with her thick dark hair shining like the river blackened by the night sky.

Almost every day this summer my sister has worn the same pair of purple corduroy shorts. She stands by the washer and dryer in her underwear waiting when our mother makes her put them in. My sister is older than me by two whole years. She knows how to braid hair and paint her toenails. She almost needs a bra. She says she will get one like her friend Lindy has—white with a little pink bow on the front. She says she will not get one like the bras our mother has—black lace with straps that come on and off. Our uncle Zack says my sister is the most beautiful girl he's ever seen. Maybe even prettier than Momma. He's right. My sister has a face like the pictures of angels that show up in big Bibles like the ones at our church where we hardly ever go. She hates that about herself. When people tell her she looks like one, she tells them they are wrong. She tells them she's a witch and then she tosses her black hair around and casts a spell on them.

My sister's slick black hair is just like our Uncle Zack's, which my mother says is a fluke. I have the same pasty pale hair that my father had when he had any and that our mother still has now.

Sometimes my sister lets me comb her hair and twist it into braids like our mother taught us. My sister's hair is smooth like the side of Mr. Albert's pony, like velvet. My sister loves her hair. Once, I put shoeshine in mine to see what it would be like to be her.

My Uncle Zack comes around on Thursdays to play cards with my father and two men from down the street. The men sit out on the back porch, the four of them huddled around the old card table that my sister and I sometimes toss a blanket over and pretend we're in a fort — waiting for the enemy to retreat. On the underside of the table my sister writes the names of the boys she likes. When she doesn't like a boy anymore she puts an X over his name. I like a boy at school named Bryce. My sister let me write his name in one of the corners. She says to be sure and X it out when I don't like him anymore. Those are the rules she says.

When the men play cards I like to hide under the porch so that I can listen to them talking. There is one place where a board is busted open and you can peek up and see the men from underneath. I like to watch them scoot their chairs and shuffle their feet when they arrange themselves to play each hand. From down under the porch they look like they are all legs and feet. Their heads are way up above and sometimes out of view so that their voices come from nowhere.

Uncle Zack and my father are brothers.

"Just like me and Annie are sisters?" I once asked my mother.

"Almost, Kiwi," she answered.

That is not my real name.

Uncle Zack and my father were also in the war together. Uncle Zack doesn't like to tell war stories, but my father does.

"In Nam," my father always starts off, "my big brother here shot every gook in his path."

"Lawrence," Uncle Zack will set down his cards and say, "you weren't even in the same platoon. What do you know?"

My father will just push off the comment with a wave of his hand and keep going.

"My brother here," he says, "he didn't take no prisoners—man, woman, or child. You should have seen him, shooting up the jungle, tearing through the thicket."

My father will make shooting noises and point his hands out like a gun as he talks. Then after a while of this, Uncle Zack always ends up slamming his beer can down on the table so that some of the gold liquid sloshes out onto the floor.

"Dammit, Lawrence," he will say, "I didn't kill no babies."

But my father just looks off into space like he's thinking of something great, shaking his head and smiling at the same time.

Today is the 4th of July. My sister says she knows why this day is important but she won't tell me. I ask Momma and she says it's because they have fireworks up at the park, which we may go to this year since Daddy is supposed to be at work at the paper mill. My sister says "fat chance." She always says "fat chance." She's usually right.

We sit outside in the yard and eat ice-cream push-ups—orange ice cream inside a tube that you push up with a plastic stick that's stuck to the bottom. They are our favorite. Uncle Zack bought them for us at the grocery store. Daddy hates them because he says we always leave their little paper toppers all around and he says we drip orange cream all through the house. Both of these things are true.

My sister says she is going off to the war and that when she gets there she will not take any prisoners either. I say that I want to go with her. She says that I am too little. She is almost a teenager she says. Twenty-seven more days and she will be thirteen. I try to act like I don't care.

Sometimes we pretend to attack the boat people. We lay down flat on the riverbank and wait.

"Quiet," my sister says to me, "they'll hear you."

I have not made a sound.

"Attack," she will say and jump up and yell at a passing boat, "attack!"

We riffle out oranges like missiles and the people on the boats wave and pass on by.

But sometimes when we play war we just hide in our fort and wait.

"When are we going to attack?" I will ask.

"Shh," my sister will say and cover my mouth with her hand, "we're hiding," she'll whisper, "the enemy will hear you."

She will peek out from time to time to see if the coast is clear.

"Not yet," she'll say softly.

If I try to peek out too she pushes me away.

"Ok," my sister will finally say, "the enemy is gone."

Around in the front I will hear my father's car start up and speed away.

Uncle Zack comes by on Saturdays when Daddy is at his second job at the paper mill. Uncle Zack rides to the grocery store with Momma and then helps her put things away. Me and my sister have to play outside while they unload all the food. It takes a long time some days.

Once I snuck back in the house and heard my mother crying.

"Jolene, now baby," Uncle Zack said to her, "there just ain't nothing we can do."

My mother sucked in a deep breath and from my spot around the corner I could see their hands on the table—Uncle Zack's big fingers stroking over my mother's little ones.

Sometimes Uncle Zack will come outside to smoke when they are finished with the groceries, and he always asks my sister to run inside and get him a cold beer. She acts like it's something special that he only asks her and I don't let on that I'm jealous. I hang around his chair and wait for her to come out with his drink. He always tells her something nice, like he likes her pigtails or how smart she is, or asks her about her plans for the summer. Sometimes I answer with my plans and he smiles at me and listens, but I'm not so little that I don't know he's waiting for me to be quiet so she will talk to him. And that's ok. I know he likes her best.

Today Daddy doesn't go to his other job at the paper mill and he and Momma have gotten in a fight about it. I hear her yelling at him.

"Lawrence," she says, "you know we need the extra money."

"That ain't all I know, Jolene."

My mother doesn't say anything more and my father comes out into the yard. I'm hiding in an orange tree but my sister is just standing out in the open, her purple shorts and red halter-top like a beacon. My father eyes her and makes a beeline straight to her. She picks up an orange off the ground and tosses it at him. It barely misses and he starts to chase her. My sister runs right to the river's edge and splashes in up to her knees. My mother comes screaming from the house and I hug the branches of my orange tree until I can't tell its limbs from my own.

My father runs down the dock and hoists himself into the raised boat. He unties the anchor and it drops to the boards below. My mother is out there with him now and she reaches for the anchor, but Daddy is down on his feet and fast. He heaves the anchor into the water, aiming at my sister. Momma screams but my sister doesn't move out of the way. The heavy anchor lands in front of her, but she doesn't flinch at all

She reaches down into the water and frees one of her oranges. On the boat dock my mother is flailing her fists at my father and in the St. John's River my sister is peeling that rotten orange and shoving slices into her mouth.

INTO THE BURN

Today my mother picks me up from school. She has a suitcase in the back seat. I ask her where we are going and she says we're going to see the world.

She hands the map to me and I spread it open. We've seen the world before. She needs to feel the ground moving beneath her, needs to see the place she is disappear behind us. She's happy on the road.

At home when she cries, her hair smells like rosemary and her skin tastes like salt. She says she cries because she's lucky and happy and sad, because she doesn't know what else to do. When I ask if there is anything I can do, she holds me tight, so tight that I know there are things in her world that aren't about me, things that break her down and make her sob.

No, sweetie, she tells me, you don't need to do anything. There is nothing you can do. I ask if I should cry too and she tells me, no, that is the last thing you should do.

She smiles, caught off guard, when I ask her, what is the first thing I should do. I love the way she looks when she smiles. The lines at her mouth and the corner of her eyes, the way the sun pales and the stars recede in comparison. There is nothing better than her smile. I live my whole life for it.

So that's why I don't mind when we see the world. Out on the road, even when we get lost, she laughs. She sings along with the radio. We stop and buy boiled peanuts from a guy by the side of the highway. Then a little tiny pumpkin from a vegetable stand. She sits the pumpkin on the dashboard and asks me if I think it will roll off.

She likes the parts of the year where the seasons change. Right now everything has turned to fall. She rolls down the window and sighs. The wind puffs in and lifts her dark hair out around her face. Something new is happening, she says, something old is floating away.

She seems hopeful but still a bit sad. I see her for a second the way she must look to people who aren't me. I think I almost see her before she knew to know me. But then it's gone. There's a picture I stole from her photo album. It's her at a football game. She looks older than I am now. She must be in college. She's smiling and her hair is much longer. She looks like a girl who looks like my mother. But in her eyes, there is someone else. In those eyes now, there's me.

When she smiles at me, the sun breaks through the clouds and lights the road ahead.

I hope we never go home.

When we get back home, I'm behind in school. I have missed a test and two assignments in Mrs. Powell's language arts class. I have to make it up by the end of the month, I say, or I don't get credit.

My mother says that I learned much more out there than they did in that classroom. I agree. I tell her, I learned that I can eat more shrimp than you can. I learned that "the pier closes at dusk" means that you have to climb over the railing to get on.

She nods and says, "We had fun, didn't we." I can almost see what she's thinking. Of the night sky and the sea blending black into each other—the stars like silver glitter flung up into the sky. And that wind, lifting her hair up and out, something new happening, something old—floating away.

I ask if she will help me with my papers. Are they about the most wonderful girl in the world, she asks. I like when she does that. One is about *Farewell to Arms*, I say, and the other is about *The Old Man and the Sea*.

She shakes her head, my goodness, doesn't Mrs. Powell know they wrote some new books in the last fifty years? What else are you reading this year, she asks. Next month, I say, we're reading *The Scarlet Letter*. She laughs in that way that people do when something is less funny and more true. She says, now there's one I can get behind.

We catch me up and she tells me that my language arts class is boring. I agree. She tells me to wait until I'm in college and then I can read the good stuff. Although, she says, I do like a man who loves cats. The next day we go to the animal shelter. We get a little gray cat and name him Ernie.

My mother doesn't have any friends. Sometimes ladies nod at her in the grocery store, but then when we're past them they smirk and whisper to each other. My mother knows they will do this and that's why she doesn't nod back to them. I have you, she tells me, and that's enough. In four years I will go to college. My mother will have only the ladies in the grocery store.

There's a man in town who I think is my father. I don't

have proof of this except that he watches me pass by on my bike with a look on his face that I don't know how to calculate. He's either my father or a pervert. Once, at the gas station we pulled up to the pump on the other side of him. He peeked at us around the tanks. My mother looked straight ahead as if there was nothing there but sky. He looked like he wanted to say something. He looked like he was sick on his stomach.

People make their choices, my mother said when we were back in the car with sodas and pretzels. I rolled down my window to let in some air.

I think when I see him again, I will wave.

Ernie likes graham crackers in milk. He does not like olives. He also does not like to be dressed in his Halloween costume. He doesn't want to greet the trick-or-treaters and put candy in their bag. He wants to be out of his cowboy outfit and under the porch. Not very many people come to our house though. I'm used to this. A lot of people drive by, but they don't stop. It's like we're famous or something. But in the wrong way.

A ballerina and Batman come up the walkway. And Brian from my geometry class. Here, he says and pushes a piece of paper in my hand. The ballerina and Batman hold their bags open for candy. Brian stands on the porch waiting for me to read the note. It says "I'm sorry." I ask Brian if this is for me and he says that his dad just told him to bring it to my house. He's a good-for-nothing, Brian says. What did he do, he asks, hit on your mom or something? I shrug my shoulders. Well, you can have him, Brian says and tugs the ballerina and Batman back out into the road.

I wonder if I can.

I put the paper in my underwear drawer. I think the

letter may be for my mother, but I hope that it's for me, so I don't tell her about it.

The day after Halloween I ride my bike past his house on the way home from school. He's out on the porch. I stop by the mailbox.

"What are you sorry about?"

He stands up quick like he's going to run inside. Instead, he walks out toward me and stops by the handlebars.

"Did you show your mother that note?"

His voice is soft and deep and sad. I shake my head.

"Good, it was for you."

I pick at the place that's wearing off on the handgrips. I don't know what to say and I guess neither does he. He digs around in his pocket and pulls out a twenty. He reaches it out to me. I take it.

"Do you know who I am?"

I nod my head and he nods back.

"I thought so."

At home, the kitchen is full of gutted pumpkins. My mother is carving a jack-o-lantern. They're all on sale, she says. Let's carve them all up and put the faces all around the yard. We'll have a séance and call up the spirits of Hemingway and Hawthorne.

Can Ernie come, I ask. He must, she says.

When it's dark we set the jack-o-lanterns around the yard. Dozens of them. Their orange faces flickering from within. My mother laughs out loud. This is the greatest thing we've ever done, she says. Don't you think?

We spread a blanket down in the midst and lay flat on our backs.

Look around, she says, it's eerie.

We're eye to eye with all the grins and grimaces. Any moment I know that something magic will happen. It must. The brown leaves rattle on the trees and there's that wind. Rolling over the pumpkin faces, kissing our foreheads, making things new. I reach in my pocket and pull out the paper. I hand it over to her. She unfolds it and holds it out in front her face. We lay there a while. She wads the paper and squeezes it tight in her hand.

Let's call out the spirits, she says and we sit up. She sits beside me and slides the nearest jack-o-lantern onto the blanket in front of us.

Put your hands up like this, she says and lifts her arms out in front of her. Like this, I ask and do the same. She clears her throat and lowers her voice. Oh stodgy spirits of language arts class, she says, show us you're here.

We giggle and she nudges me to play along. I put on my best, fake séance voice. Give us a sign. Will I get an A on my paper?

Ernie comes racing around the side of the house and stops in his tracks. He creeps up on the fat pumpkin under the tree, sticks his nose inside the mouth and jumps back away from the flame. He runs off through the jack-o-lantern maze and disappears under the fence. My mother looks at me. Hemingway, she says and nods knowingly.

We giggle and call up the ghosts some more. After a while she opens her hand and holds out the ball of paper.

"Do you know who he is?"

I nod.

"I thought so."

She gives the paper to me.

"You can talk to him if you want."

I nod and fold the paper in a neat square. I reach it out toward the glowing mouth in front of me. I slip the paper into the smile. Smoke lifts from the eyes and the cut around the stem, then drifts off into the breeze.

Something new is happening. Something old is floating away.

AMY WILLOUGHBY-BURLE was raised in the small coastal town of Kure Beach, North Carolina. She graduated with a BA in English and an unfinished Masters in Creative Writing ("sorry Mom and Dad") from East Carolina University. She spent several years in her husband's home state of Missouri before getting homesick for North Carolina and her family and now lives in the mountains near Asheville with her very gracious husband and three children. Her fiction has appeared in numerous literary journals, such as *Potomac Review, Inkwell, Sycamore Review, Reed Magazine, The MacGuffin,* and others.

Visit Amy online at: www.amywilloughbyburle.com.

Cover artist **KEVIN ADAMS** is a naturalist, writer, teacher, and photographer. He has had a lifelong love affair with nature and the outdoors, particularly the mountains and coast in his home state of North Carolina. A photographer for more than 25 years, Kevin is the author of nine books, including the bestselling *North Carolina Waterfalls.* He also writes magazine articles and his photographs appear regularly in books, magazines, calendars, and advertisements across the country. Kevin has traveled extensively, particularly in North Carolina where, in addition to photography, he enjoys hiking, kayaking, and gazing up at the night sky. He lives in the mountains of western North Carolina with his lovely wife, Patricia, their mischievous cats, Lucy and Titan, and a host of critters who regularly pop in for a visit. A groundhog, who lives under their house, likes to eat Patricia's flowers.

Kevin says of the cover image: "Making this photo gave me the chance to be a kid again. As a child, I loved catching fireflies and putting them in a jar. As an adult photographer, I relived that experience. After catching about a dozen of the little buggers with my butterfly net, I put them in a jar and set it on a wicker table on my front porch. I focused the camera on the jar and set it to shoot continuous 15-second exposures at a high ISO. Then I went to sleep for a couple of hours while the camera ran. Back at the camera, I refocused on the sky and then shot one exposure to capture the Milky Way. During this exposure, I saw the biggest meteor flash I had ever seen. I was astounded, but it took me a few seconds to realize that not only was I blessed to witness such an event, but that I had captured it with my camera! Back at the computer, I discovered that of the hundreds of exposures made for the jar, 55 of them showed firefly flashes. I combined these with the Milky Way exposure to create the final photograph."

You can find more of Kevin's work at: www.kadamsphoto.com, and on his *Digital After Dark* blog at www.kadamsphoto.com/nightphotography.

FROM THE AUTHOR

All my love and gratitude to my family. To my parents and brother and sister who shaped my world in all the right ways. Thank you to my wonderful husband, RJ, who is ever supportive and encouraging of my writing and makes my world a happy place. And thanks to my children, who are "the heavens and the seas."

Many thanks to the people who have encouraged and inspired me and made me fall in love with storytelling. I feel lucky to have had so many writers and readers in my life who have provided both critique and companionship. Special thanks to Luke Whisnant, my teacher and friend, the many writers and faculty instructors at Wildacres Writers Workshop, the ladies and gentlemen of Saturday Writers in St. Peters, Missouri, and many others. I've been blessed to be a part of some wonderful writers critique groups and I believe those relationships to be invaluable.

Finally and most importantly, I thank God for any talent I might have in this endeavor. He didn't give me math skills or any ability to understand the laws of physics, and perhaps not as much common sense as I could sometimes use, but He did give me a wild imagination and a love of language and literature. So to Him and all the people in my life who support me, I am eternally grateful.

www.ingramcontent.com/pod-product-compliance
Lightning Source LLC
Chambersburg PA
CBHW030354180626
46812CB00007B/2884